D1255494

AFTER DARK

Other books by Cynthia Danielewski:

Edge of Night

AFTER DARK

•

Cynthia Danielewski

AVALON BOOKS
NEW YORK

PRINTED IN THE UNITED STATES OF AMERICA
ON ACID-FREE PAPER
BY HADDON CRAFTSMEN, BLOOMSBURG, PENNSYLVANIA

For Jim, Janice, and Christa.

Chapter One

The wedding reception was in full swing at the quaint bed-and-breakfast located in the historic district of St. Augustine, Florida. The tiny white lights that adorned the trees glistened in the misty night air as a small band played romantic melodies from the past.

Daniel Gallows cast a quick glance at his watch and left the dance area in search of some peace and quiet. It was almost midnight. The night's festivities had been under way for well over three hours, and he needed a respite from the noise of the crowd. He wanted the opportunity to regroup before he was called upon to mingle again. It was his only niece's wedding, and all of his energy had been focused on making sure that the night was perfect for her.

As he walked around the perimeter of the property, he noticed a wrought iron bench nestled under a large tree. The small seating area seemed far enough away from the boisterous crowd so that he could gather his thoughts, but close enough in case he was needed. It looked like the ideal place to smoke. Wanting a few minutes of solitude before his niece noticed that he was missing, he made his way over to the bench.

He felt some of his tension dissipate as he walked away from the noise of the party. The temperature of the air seemed cooler away from the lights and the crowd, and he raised his face slightly to the breeze in an effort to take advantage of the refreshing light wind. Reaching into his suit jacket, he removed a pack of cigarettes and a lighter.

He was just about to light the tip of his cigarette when he felt a presence from behind. He turned, ready to greet one of the wedding guests. His smile of welcome faded the moment he realized he was alone.

An unsettling feeling washed over him as the light fog blanketing the ground swirled around him like a shroud. He peered through the shadowy mist, pinpricks of apprehension assaulting him, and tried to determine what had disturbed him. But as his eyes searched the immediate vicinity, all he could see or hear were the wedding guests enjoying the night. He glanced around one final time before he turned and settled back in his seat.

Lighting the tip of his cigarette, he closed his eyes and took a deep drag. The events of the day flooded his mind, and a small smile touched his lips as he thought about how everything seemed to go off without a hitch. The weather cooperated. The night was warm and balmy, allowing the guests to enjoy the outside dance pavilion that had been set up. Even the light evening fog had not put a damper on the day's festivities.

He was lost in his own thoughts when he felt the

icy touch of a hand on the back of his neck. Startled, his eyes popped open. "What . . ." he managed to get out before a tight vise wrapped itself around his throat, cutting off the words.

Chapter Two

In the early morning hours, Detective John Delaney was driving home when his cell phone rang. Reaching out, he lowered the volume on the radio before answering the call. "Delaney."

The slight sound of static came over the line before he heard his name growled. "John?"

John recognized the caller immediately. It was Frank Capelli, the captain of police for St. Augustine, Florida. "Hi, Frank," he greeted, wondering why the man felt the necessity to track him down. A glance at the digital clock illuminated on the dashboard assured him that this wasn't a social call. He silently groaned at the thought. He had just spent the last five hours with a group of college kids, explaining the benefits and personal rewards of a career in law enforcement. The last thing he wanted to deal with was the petty crimes that seemed to plague the city lately. At the moment, the only thing he wanted was sleep.

"John, are you there?" the voice growled as the cell phone's reception faded for a moment.

"Yeah, Frank. I'm here. What's up?"

"What's your location?" Frank asked without pre-amble, not bothering with niceties.

John frowned at the urgency in Frank's tone of voice. "I'm on the outskirts of town. Why?"

"A body was found at the old Pritchard place in the historic district."

John was shocked into silence by the words. It was the last thing he expected to hear. The feeling of fatigue that he had been experiencing abruptly vanished as he thought about Frank's statement. The historic district of St. Augustine catered mostly to tourists, and the streets were usually heavy with foot traffic as people explored the attractions of the nation's oldest city. The hour wasn't late enough for the area to be deserted, and the city normally didn't have a problem with violent crime. "The Pritchard place? I thought that house was converted into a bed-and-breakfast sometime last year."

"It was. It's called Crosswind now. The place caters to wealth. As a matter of fact, the murder took place during a wedding reception."

"You're kidding," John said, disbelief evident in his voice.

An audible sigh came over the phone line. "I wish I was. Can you meet me and McNeal there?"

John glanced at the clock on the dashboard once more. "Sure. No problem. Give me about fifteen minutes."

"You got it. I'll see you in a bit," Frank said before hanging up.

John flipped the cell phone shut and placed it back on the dashboard. Casting a quick look in his rearview mirror, he changed lanes before making a U-turn and heading toward the bed-and-breakfast.

As he drove along the interstate, he thought about Frank's words regarding the location and time of the homicide. Both seemed out of place, out of sync, with the normal scenarios usually found. Unless the action was that of a hit, John didn't believe that this was a meaningless act. There was no way it could be. The location was too open, the field of witnesses too heavy.

He tried to think of a connection between the scene of the crime and a probable motive. Searching his memory, he vaguely recalled reading an article on the renovation of Crosswind in the local paper, but he couldn't recollect any of the details. The fact didn't really surprise him. He had never followed any news that took place in the society pages. His lifestyle didn't run in those circles. When his wife, Caitlin, had passed away from a brain tumor several years back, he had immersed himself in his work in an effort to deal with his grief. At the time, he didn't have the inclination to socialize. And as the days went by, what started out as a coping mechanism became his way of life. With the exception of a few friends, he pretty much kept to himself. Which for the most part, suited him fine. It was only when things like this happened that he wished he had a better grasp on the social scene within the city.

Seeing his exit up ahead, John flipped on his turn

signal. He followed the trail of flashing lights from the emergency vehicles that had been dispatched to the site. Heading down San Marco Avenue, he passed the Castillo De San Marcos, noting that the impressive coquina rock fort situated on Matanzas Bay still had tourists mulling around the outside grounds, though the National Monument was closed for the evening. The sight wasn't anything unusual. There were still people walking around the popular area that was located in the heart of the historic district, commuting from the City Gates as they looked for areas of interest to investigate. The old tombstones and crypts of Huguenot Cemetery seemed to hold strong appeal, as visitors lined up outside the locked gates, listening with rapt interest while costumed tour guides gave detailed lectures on the rich history of the city under the guise of a ghost tour. John knew that the heavy promotion of the tours breathed a new cycle of nightlife into the city, guaranteeing that the streets would stay busy well into the early morning hours. And ordinarily, that wasn't a problem. But tonight it meant that the crime scene would have more spectators than normal as people's natural curiosity took hold.

He gave the people he passed a fleeting glance, his attention focused on the job at hand. Turning down a side street, he saw the flashing lights up ahead that told him he had arrived at Crosswind.

Reporters were already set up by the black wrought iron gate that surrounded the property, and cameramen were jockeying for position outside the police barricade, trying to capture the images of the crime scene. John shook his head slightly at the sight, wondering briefly at the fascination the press seemed to have with death. The fascination that people had with death in general. He noticed that the tourists were getting in on the action, just as expected. Several costumed tour guides affiliated with the night tours, stood with their groups in the recesses of the shadows, watching the commotion from afar.

Driving his car through the gate that led to the front entrance of the house, John stopped briefly to flash his badge to the rookie officer directing traffic. After getting clearance, he parked under the leaves of an old oak tree, joining the numerous patrol cars that were already on site.

The heat and humidity of the July night washed over him in waves the moment he stepped from the air conditioned vehicle, and he ran a weary hand through his short black hair as he tried to adjust to the sudden change in temperature. He looked into the back seat of his car to where his suit jacket lay. He debated briefly as to whether or not to don it. The hot weather was oppressive, and the idea of wearing an extra layer of clothing held no appeal. But as quickly as he contemplated the idea, he discarded it. His ingrained sense of professionalism refused to allow him to concede to personal comfort. Reaching into the car for his jacket, he shrugged into it before adjusting the knot of his tie.

As he stood by the car, he took the time to familiarize himself with the layout of the estate and the actions of the people surrounding him. The house itself was an old Victorian, typical of the houses that were so popular in the area. The unadorned windows sparkled under the porch lights, allowing him a glimpse inside. He could see the gleaming woodwork through the clear glass panes, the animated faces of the guests as they spoke amongst themselves. Forcing his eyes away from the commotion going on inside the residence, he continued to look around the property that had been professionally landscaped to resemble an English garden. When he noticed a group of people working in the backyard, he walked around the perimeter of the grounds to where they stood.

He thought about Frank's remark that a wedding reception had taken place that night, and he couldn't help but catch a glimpse of the truth of that statement. The tiny white lights that hung like garland on the trees still shimmered in the night, while wedding guests formally dressed waited impatiently on the sidelines, awaiting their turn to talk to the police officers assigned to take statements.

John looked around the area with interest, but as he walked closer to a group of officers talking amongst themselves, all of his attention focused on the ground where the body lay draped in a pristine white sheet.

Acknowledging the officers' presence, he went down on his haunches and reached for the edge of the sheet. Gripping it firmly between his fingers, he pulled it down to get his first glimpse of the victim. He was unprepared for the sight that greeted him.

Eyes that were cold and lifeless stared back at him unseeingly, and a slightly bluish cast overshadowed the victim's features, leaving a discernible impression on the night that was still shadowed by a light fog. His gaze traveled over the victim's face before fixating on the telltale signs of strangulation that were deeply embedded in the victim's neck. He was staring at the abrasions when he heard the sound of footsteps from behind. Instinctively he placed the sheet back over the body before turning. His eyebrows rose slightly when he saw his partner, Sam McNeal.

"Hi," Sam greeted, covering a yawn behind his hand.

"Hi," John replied, rising from his crouched position. His eyes studied Sam in the floodlights that the police had placed around the property so that the CSI team could work. He noticed the unkempt sandy-colored hair of his partner, and the wrinkled cloth of his suit. Though his partner was no male model, he almost always was dressed to impress. The fact that he looked like he had slept in his clothes had John looking at him curiously. "Rough night?"

Sam sighed and ran a weary hand over his eyes. "Who would have thought that a baby wouldn't sleep. I thought that was all they were supposed to do."

John smiled. Sam's wife, Elizabeth, had recently given birth to their first born child, and he knew they were having a rough time making the adjustment to the new addition in their life. Though it was obvious the baby was the most important thing to the two of them, he also knew from recent talks with Sam that the baby's sleep patterns seemed to be on a different schedule than either of his parents. "Things will get easier," John assured him.

"I hope so," Sam replied. Reaching into the inside pocket of his suit, he brought out his wire-rimmed glasses and donned them. "I wasn't sure if Frank had been able to reach you."

"I was on my way home when he called. It was easy enough to make a U-turn and head over here."

Sam looked at John, noticing his bloodshot eyes and

his short hair that was standing slightly on end. "You look like you had a rough night, too."

"You try spending an entire evening with a bunch of college kids after a long day at work."

Sam smiled. "A little rowdy, were they?"

"That's an understatement."

Sam smirked. "Well, it's over now and it was for a good cause. You can take comfort in the fact that you did your civic duty."

"Yeah, well, next year it's your turn."

"I would have done it this year if it weren't for Elizabeth and the baby. You know my household has been hectic lately."

John rolled his eyes at the words. "Just remember, you can only use that excuse once. Don't even think about asking me to cover for you next year. I'll need at least a couple of years to recuperate from tonight."

Sam laughed. "All kidding aside, how was the seminar?"

John shrugged. "All right, I guess. The college kids seemed genuinely interested in police procedure. After they settled down that is. I can't honestly say the night was a waste."

"Let's hope your speech had the desired effect and we'll be able to recruit a few of them."

"That was the plan."

Sam grunted in reply and reached for the sheet to examine the body. His full attention was now focused on the corpse. "Whoa!"

"I think I had the same reaction when I saw him."

"Strangulation?"

"Looks that way," John replied just as he caught sight of a shoe impression on the wet grass. Moving closer to get a better look, his eyes were immediately drawn to the pointed indention of the heel pattern, indicating that the print belonged to a woman. He absently bent down to trace the mark with his finger.

Sam watched his action. "Spike heels?"

"Definitely."

Sam glanced back to the patio to where the wedding guests were being detained. "I'm sure a lot of women here are wearing shoes with that type of heel."

"Probably. But we should make a cast of it just to be on the safe side. You never know if we'll need it to prove the identity of the killer," John said, stepping back to allow the photographer to get close-up shots of the impression.

"As soon as they get done snapping the photos, we'll get someone here to pour the cast."

"We'll need to get it done as soon as possible. The ground is soft from the moisture of the night. I don't want to take a chance that the dirt will start to pack into the indention," John said.

Sam nodded slightly, agreeing with the assessment. He looked up, catching sight of Frank Capelli. "Here comes Frank."

"I'm glad you two could make it," Frank said as he walked up to them. He motioned with his chin to the body. "What do you think?"

John ignored the question, instead asking one of his own. "Who's the victim?"

"Daniel Gallows," Frank said, not taking offense at the side step. He knew John well enough to know that his thought pattern was methodical. It was one of the reasons that he was such a good cop. He never rushed a judgment. He liked to have some basic answers before he gave any theories, and Frank couldn't fault him for it. John's success rate for solving cases was the highest of all the detectives in the precinct, and Frank was grateful that he chose to stay in the city to work. He knew that with his qualifications, he could have gotten a job anywhere in the country.

John mentally digested the name, trying to remember if he had ever heard it mentioned before. He didn't think he had. "Who found the body?" he asked, turning to look at the harried expressions of the guests from the party as the uniformed officers interviewed them.

"The bride, Christine Gallows," Frank said.

John nodded. "Any relation to the victim?"

"She was his niece," Frank replied.

Sam let out a soft whistle. "Nice way to end your special day."

Frank sighed. "You can say that again."

Sam looked at Frank. "Have you had a chance to talk to any of the guests?"

Frank inclined his head slightly and stepped back as the forensics team combed the area for evidence. "A few."

"Did anything noteworthy pop up?" Sam asked.

"Just the basics," Frank replied before motioning to the body. "You think this could have been a random killing?"

"By strangulation? Come on, you know better than that," John scoffed. "Of all the easy ways to take someone out, strangulation has to be one of the most difficult. It's not an easy method for anybody to carry out."

Sam lifted a shoulder expressively. "I have to admit,

I agree with John. There are definitely easier ways to kill someone."

Frank's gaze encompassed both men. "Easier? How?"

John shrugged. "Think about it. If the right amount of pressure wasn't applied to the air passage of the victim, the murder wouldn't have been successful. The killer had to have a basic knowledge of human anatomy. Without knowing exactly where to constrict the windpipe, the only thing they might have been able to accomplish was to inflict some nasty wounds to the neck. But he or she would have had to deal with the gasping for air that the victim would have been struggling for. And that's not always a quiet process."

"Especially if the victim fought," Sam pointed out.

John glanced down at the body. "Which is pretty much a given. It would have been an instinctive action for Gallows to struggle. Which also means, that our suspect would have to be strong enough to hold their own against someone of Gallows's size."

"If I was taking a guess, I would say that we're looking for a man," Sam said, motioning to Daniel Gallows. "He's no lightweight."

"No, he's not," John agreed. "But the killer would have had the element of surprise on his side. You can't underestimate the power of that. If the murderer was able to approach Gallows undetected and struck the first blow, he would have automatically gained the upper hand in the attack."

Frank was quiet for a moment as he thought about John's words. "So you don't believe this was an arbitrary act."

"Hardly," John replied. "There has to be some sort

of meaning to this particular action. Strangulation isn't a quick out. It's a slow, painful one."

"And?" Frank prompted.

"I think we're dealing with someone who had a definite vendetta against the victim. There's no way that this could have been a chance killing. It had to be planned. At a guess, I would say that whoever our killer was followed Daniel Gallows throughout the night. They knew exactly when to make their move so that their actions wouldn't be detected," John said.

"Following him around would have been risky," Sam murmured as he considered John's theory.

"I agree. Murdering someone in the midst of a party definitely takes some guts," Frank said.

John nodded in agreement. "I'm not arguing with that. And that alone gives us the first clue as to what type of person we're dealing with."

"What do you mean?" Sam asked.

"I think we're searching for someone with cold-blooded tendencies. This wasn't a crime of passion. It wasn't some person passing by the gate who decided then and there that he was going to end someone's life. It was calculated. The murderer had to derive a certain amount of satisfaction at being able to pull this off. Especially considering the amount of people that were here tonight. The sense of accomplishment that they have to be feeling now is going to outweigh any hint of conscience they may have experienced after actually committing the murder. That fact by itself is going to make them a dangerous adversary. If they were able to commit this act and get away undetected, they're going to believe that they're invincible."

16   *Cynthia Danielewski*

"And they might think that they're going to get away with it," Frank murmured to himself.

"Only if we let them," John replied.

Sam glanced at the people detained on the patio. "You think it could have been one of the wedding guests?"

John inclined his head. "I would say that was a distinct possibility. Looking at the marks embedded in the victim's neck, the cord used to cut off his flow of air was thin in width. I'm sure that whatever object was used to kill Daniel Gallows was easy enough for anybody to keep on their person undetected."

"It's possible that the murderer wasn't involved with the wedding. They could have just been biding their time to get to Gallows," Sam said.

"That's doubtful," John replied.

Sam glanced around the yard, noting the small side gate that led to the street. He motioned in its direction. "It probably would have been easy enough for someone to get to him by either coming or leaving by that gate."

John followed his gaze. "Possible, but unlikely. How long does a wedding reception usually take? Four, possibly five hours? The idea of someone laying in wait for the man to move off into the shadows isn't feasible. Not with this many people about. Not with the amount of traffic that's usually on the street."

"It's feasible if the person's psychotic," Frank said.

John smiled slightly, but the smile held no humor. "If I were a betting man, I wouldn't take the odds."

"It's possible that the murderer believed the fog tonight would allow them to get away undetected. It's possible they were a betting man or woman, which-ever the case may be," Sam pointed out.

"Anything's possible," John acknowledged wryly. "I still wouldn't bet the bank on it."

"So, where do we start?" Sam asked.

John looked at Frank. "What do we know about what took place here tonight?"

Frank shrugged. "Not much, I'm afraid. The victim, Daniel Gallows, was heavy in real estate. Probably had enough money to buy whatever caught his fancy. His niece, Christine, was the one person he stayed close to. Her father had passed away when she was younger, and I guess he acted as a surrogate father."

"So money's a possible motive," Sam said.

Frank nodded. "Bridget Gallows, the bride's mother, was out of favor with the uncle. Apparently she has expensive tastes and looked to him to support her buying habits. I got the distinct impression from what I've been able to find out so far, that if it weren't for the niece, Mrs. Gallows would have been cut off from any monetary support long ago."

"And the groom?" John asked, watching as the coroner's van backed up to the area to remove the body.

"Brad Paxton. His own family has wealth, but you know what they say. You can never be too rich or too thin. The fact that he is now officially married to what I'm going to assume is Daniel Gallows's heir, has put him in a very favorable position in life," Frank said.

"So far, the only motive I'm hearing is greed," Sam said.

Frank nodded. "It does seem to be shaping up that way."

"Did anything show on any business partners?" John asked.

"Nothing as of yet. What I have is just preliminary information we were able to obtain from the guests present tonight. It seems loyalty to the Gallows family is pretty much nonexistent if the way these people spoke about them is any indication," Frank replied.

John glanced at the patio. "What about the proprietor of this place?"

"We don't have too much on her. There's one sole owner. A woman. She said she was walking the grounds, ensuring that the guests were all being taken care of, when she stumbled upon Christine Gallows standing over her uncle," Frank said.

"Did she say if anything looked suspicious?" John asked.

Frank shook his head slightly. "She stated at first glance she thought the man may have just passed out. From too much alcohol or from the heat, she wasn't sure. It wasn't until she saw the expression on the niece's face that she realized something else was up."

"Did she say if the niece said anything suspicious or out of character for the situation?" Sam asked.

"No," Frank replied. "As a matter of fact, that was one of the first questions I asked. She said Christine Gallows was bordering on hysterics when she found her. To her, it seemed like a natural enough reaction."

"What was your feeling of the woman?" John asked, staring at the ground. Though the victim's body had been removed, the wet dew of the grass had acted as a mold. The imprint of the body was still noticeable upon the soft earth, the impression out of place on the manicured grounds.

"The proprietor?" Frank clarified.

John forced his attention back to the conversation. "Yeah."

Frank's forehead creased into a frown as he thought about the question. "She seemed okay. A little shook up by what occurred, but overall handling it well. She runs the place by herself. I would imagine that she has to have pretty good coping skills dealing with the public like she does."

"What's her name?" John asked, wondering if he would have heard it around. Though he usually stayed clear of the tourist areas of town, he had countless business connections. There was always the possibility that the name would ring a bell.

"Mary Jones. Sound familiar?"

John searched his memory. "I can't say I know her," he replied just as Henry Lark, the team leader of the CSI team, walked toward them.

Frank watched him approach. "Did you find something?"

Henry inclined his head. "I believe we may have found the murder weapon."

Chapter Three

John glanced in the direction of where Henry had just come from, his eyes scanning the area. "Where?"

"In the shrubs over there," Henry said, making a gesture with his hand in the general direction of where the item was found.

John's gaze followed the motion. "What is it?"

Henry grimaced. "A strip of leather. The one thing that's guaranteed not to break. There's no way it would have accidentally snapped while being wrapped around Gallows's neck."

"How did you find it?" Frank asked.

"It was buried in the thicket, and from what I can tell, it was deliberately placed there. If it weren't for the floodlights that we're using, it definitely would have been overlooked. The shrub's in full bloom. The leather and the bark of the branches resemble one another."

Sam looked at him curiously. "What makes you think it was deliberately placed there?"

Henry shrugged. "It appears to have been neatly coiled, as if someone carefully set it down on the ground. If it had been carelessly thrown, the chances of it being in that position would have been slim."

John left the trio of men, wanting to get a look at the object in question. Walking over to the area where the item was discovered, he went down on his haunches to get a closer look at the potential piece of evidence.

At first glance, the long piece of black leather looked innocuous, similar to a tie that could have been used for the planting of new trees in the garden. He mentally took note of the size. It was about thirty inches long and about a fourth of an inch wide.

Henry walked up beside John. "What do you think?"

"What makes you think this could be the murder weapon?" John asked absently as he reached for the small penlight flashlight he carried in the inside pocket of his suit. Flicking the instrument on, he shone the light on the ground, looking for something, anything that would possibly support Henry's theory.

Henry bent down next to him. Reaching for his own flashlight, he shone the beam on the object. "You see that discoloration?"

John squinted, trying to see what Henry had just pointed out with the beam of light. When his eyes caught sight of the slight color difference on the strip of material, he nodded. "Yeah."

Henry kept his light trained on the object long enough for Sam and Frank to get a glimpse of the evidence. "Something touched the leather that left a stain."

Sam's forehead creased into a frown as he stared at the discoloration. "That could be anything. Including the dew from the grass."

Henry inclined his head slightly. "That's true, but there's also the distinct possibility that it's sweat, or even blood for that matter. There were a couple of wounds in the victim's neck that drew a few droplets."

"You think that's fluid evidence?" Frank asked.

"That's what I'm hoping," Henry said. "Once we get it to the lab, we'll be able to have it analyzed to determine exactly what it is. The marks on the victim's neck are pretty close in width to this piece."

"We'll need an exact measurement to be sure that it's the actual murder weapon," Frank said.

"We'll be able to get an exact measurement after all the data is collected and analyzed," Henry assured him.

"Maybe we'll luck out and this piece of material will have some DNA evidence on it," Sam murmured.

"I think we'll be able to get an exact match to the victim," Henry said, his voice full of confidence. "With regards to the perpetrator, it'll depend on how careless they were."

John looked at the distance between where the article of evidence had been found and the location of where the victim's body had been discovered. "This is in the opposite direction of the gate. As a matter of fact, if you follow this trail, chances are that our murderer went back into the midst of the crowd."

Sam followed his gaze. "Lending support to the theory that the killer is still among us."

John stared at the people on the patio. "The question remains, whose motive is the strongest?"

"I think that's going to be the toughest part of the puzzle to fit. The field is heavy with suspects, and we haven't even scratched the surface of this investigation," Sam reminded him.

"I know. We'll have to keep in mind that the psychological aspects of the killer's thought process are going to play a heavy role in eliminating individuals as possible suspects," John said.

"So how do you want to proceed?" Frank asked.

John rubbed a weary hand across the back of his neck and cast a quick glance at his watch. "The way I see it, we have only one option. We'll have to investigate the major players to see where the road leads. And there's no time like the present to start."

Thirty minutes later, John escorted Christine Gallows into the parlor of the bed-and-breakfast. Sam was in the adjoining room talking to her husband, while Frank was with her mother.

As John walked behind Christine, he couldn't help but think of the difficulty he had in getting her to agree to talk to him without her husband present. She was definitely nervous. John had managed to convince her that the interview would go much more quickly if their statements were taken individually. The reality was, he didn't want to give them any chance to collaborate their stories. He knew people had a tendency to be more truthful when confronted alone.

Once they were in the brightly-lit parlor, he motioned for her to have a seat on the cream-colored sofa. He watched her carefully as she got settled, noting her physical appearance and demeanor. The fact that she was upset was obvious. Her light brown hair was in

disarray, and little rivulets of black mascara were noticeable on her face, the streaks caused by tears. But
it was her behavior that he was the most interested in.
He couldn't help but notice that she shifted uncomfortably in his presence. He didn't know why. While
it would have been normal for her to be a little nervous, the apprehension that she was displaying seemed
excessive considering the circumstances. And considering her relationship to the victim. "Would you like
a glass of water before we begin?" he asked, trying to
put her at ease.

Christine Gallows took a deep shuddering breath
before she responded. "No. I'm fine."

John nodded and took a seat opposite her. Her rest-
less movements brought his attention to the dirt that
was noticeable around the hemline of her gown. The
sight gave validation to the fact that she had been out
in the garden that evening. "I know this has been a
difficult time for you," he began, his tone of voice low
and soothing as he tried to gain her confidence.

Christine looked at him with tear-filled eyes, her
hands nervously playing with a lace handkerchief that
she clutched. "It has been."

"Could you tell me when was the last time you saw
your uncle alive?" he asked her gently.

She dabbed at her eyes with the handkerchief and
took a shaky breath. "I guess shortly before midnight.
We had just finished cutting the cake."

"At the time, did anything seem out of place to
you?"

"Out of place?" she repeated, her brow wrinkled in
uncertainty as if he was speaking a foreign language.
"I don't understand what you mean by that."

"That's all right," John assured her, hearing the note of panic in her voice. His objective was to keep her calm, to keep her talking. "I need to know if your uncle seemed normal to you. Was he agitated in any way? Upset?"

She shook her head vehemently. "No. He seemed fine. As a matter of fact, we were joking that something was probably going to go wrong any minute."

John looked at her in confusion, not understanding the meaning of her words. To him, the comment seemed odd and out of place considering it was her wedding day. "Why would you think that something was going to go wrong?"

"Because the day had been so perfect," she said, her tone of voice indicating that she believed it was a natural comment. She abruptly jumped up from her chair and began to pace on the small area rug, absently reaching up to push a few tendrils of hair behind her ear. The action knocked out a pin that had been used to secure her veil, and it fell silently to the carpet. She didn't seem to notice. "I don't understand how this could have happened. I don't understand why this happened. He was a good man. He didn't deserve this."

"No, he didn't," John agreed, biting back the words that nobody deserved this. He didn't want to get philosophical. He was grateful that she was talking. That was the important thing. And the fact that she was doing it without any prodding from him gave him hope that she would say something that would help them solve this case. He waited patiently for her to begin speaking again.

She continued to pace the small room, her steps allowing him a glimpse of her shoes. He looked at them curiously, wanting to see the type of heel. They were flats.

"Why would someone do this to him?" she asked forlornly, her breath catching on a sob.

"I don't know. Did he have any enemies that you were aware of? Anybody that would have something to gain from his death?" he asked, making sure that he kept any hint of threat out of his voice.

She paused for a moment, thinking seriously about his question. "He's been on the phone a lot lately with someone. He seemed angry with the person on the other end of the line."

"Who was it?"

"I don't know," she said, her voice barely a whisper.

John sat forward in his seat so that he could hear her better. "You didn't hear any names mentioned?"

"No."

"What about the conversations? Did he always seem to be upset when he spoke to this person?"

"Not always. Sometimes he would laugh. It seemed a little strange," she murmured, her voice trailing off.

"What did?" he prompted.

"His mood swings."

"What was his normal temperament?"

She dabbed at her eyes once again as her tears freely began to flow. "He was always a little straight-laced, that was his nature. But whenever he talked to this person, he seemed to become agitated. At the time, I didn't think anything of it. There's a lot of pressure in his business."

"He was in real estate, wasn't he?"

She nodded absently. "Among other things. He liked to dabble."

"What were his other interests? Maybe there's something there that will help us locate the murderer."

"He owned part of an art gallery, and a couple of car dealerships. He was on the board of trustees at the bank."

"Would you be able to come up with a list of his associates?"

She looked at him, her blue eyes still shimmering with tears that were ready to fall. "I can do that. All I have to do is give you a copy of the guest list. Most of his associates were invited here tonight, though not all of them showed up."

"Do you know all of these people personally?"

"No. I only know most of them by name."

"Then if you don't mind my asking, why would you invite people to your wedding that you don't know?"

"My uncle believed that you should keep your friends close and your enemies closer. He wanted everybody he knew to get an invitation. I didn't have the heart to tell him no."

John nodded slightly, absorbing her comment about her uncle wanting to keep his enemies close. She may not have realized it, but that comment just widened the scope that the investigation would have to take. "If you would give us a copy of the guest list, it would be a great help."

"I'll get it for you as soon as possible," she promised.

"You had mentioned earlier that your uncle seemed agitated during the telephone calls. Could you be a little more specific?"

She took a deep breath, trying to think of the best

way to describe what she had witnessed. "His voice would start to rise, almost as if he was shouting."

"Some people speak differently on a telephone than face-to-face. Could that have been his normal telephone persona?"

She gave a shaky laugh. "Hardly."

John looked at her curiously. "How would you describe him then?"

"You mean, how would I describe his behavior on a daily basis?"

"Yes."

Christine shrugged and walked over to a small portable bar that had been set up by the fireplace. Reaching for the crystal pitcher of water that rested on the top, she poured a small amount into a glass before taking a sip. "Daniel loved life."

"He was an extrovert?"

"You could say that. He was always on the go. He wasn't a homebody by any stretch of the imagination."

"Was he seeing anybody romantically?"

"You mean dating?"

John nodded. "Yes."

Christine thought about his question for a moment before answering. "To be honest, I'm not really sure."

"You're not sure?" he asked, looking at her suspiciously. From what he could gather so far, she seemed to be relatively close to her uncle. He couldn't fathom that she wouldn't know if her uncle had a girlfriend.

Christine took another audible breath and walked back over to the sofa. "I know it sounds strange, but I honestly don't know."

"He never mentioned anybody?"

"Not to me. His personal life wasn't something we

discussed. Maybe it was due to the fact that he always considered me a kid. My father died when I was young, and I think my uncle tried to fill his shoes to a certain extent."

"That's understandable," John said, trying to instill the right amount of understanding in his voice to keep her talking.

"My uncle was very good to me," she assured him.

"I'm sure he was."

"There wasn't anything he wouldn't do for me."

"I believe that."

"I owe him a great deal. I'll do anything I can to help you find his killer," Christine vowed just as the door to the parlor was abruptly thrown open.

Chapter Four

Both John and Christine turned at the sound.

"Christine!" called a male voice.

"Brad!" she exclaimed, startled by the interruption. "What's the matter? Did something else happen?"

John inwardly sighed at the intrusion, knowing that his interview with Christine Gallows was going to come abruptly to an end. He tried to keep the frustration from his voice as he stood. "Brad Paxton?"

"That's right," Brad said, his eyes sizing John up.

"I'm Detective John Delaney."

"I know who you are."

John studied the man silently, noting his stance. Though not outwardly aggressive, there was a certain defensiveness to his stature, a guarded look in his eyes. "Have we met before?" he asked, trying to recall if he had ever met the guy. His memory came up blank.

"No, we've never met," Brad replied, not expanding on the statement.

"Then how do you know who he is?" Christine asked after a moment of silence.

He glanced in her direction, his eyes softening. "The other detective told me," he admitted, noticing the evidence of tears in her eyes. "Are you okay?"

"Detective Delaney was just asking me some questions about Daniel."

Brad nodded and crossed over to stand beside his wife. "You don't mind if I hang around, do you?" he asked, addressing the question to John.

John knew it was irrelevant if he did mind. He had the distinct impression that the man wasn't going anywhere unless he was forcefully removed. "We were just about through."

"Good. Then I'm not interrupting anything," Brad replied.

"Not at all," John assured him, wondering why the man felt the need to be nearby during his wife's questioning. He had a feeling that the reasoning behind his presence went beyond normal husbandly concern. He considered Brad Paxton carefully. His obvious discomfort with his wife's interview seemed out of proportion to the events of the evening. He automatically glanced at the man's feet, noting the little blades of grass that had dried on the top portion of his shoes. He wondered when the man had taken a stroll on the grounds.

"Don't let me keep you from continuing," Brad said.

"As I said, we were just about through," John replied, reaching into his suit jacket for a business card. He held it out to Christine. "If you can think of anything else that you believe might be helpful with the investigation, please call me."

Christine reached for the card. "I will."

Brad looked at John and took his wife's hand. "Then if that's all you need, we'll get out of your way. I'm sure you have other people that you need to talk to."

Christine's eyes met John's. "My husband and I want to help in any way we can with the investigation."

John inclined his head. "Of course."

"I'll get that guest list to you as soon as possible," she promised.

"Thank you," John said.

"You're welcome," she replied before her husband led her from the room.

John watched them leave.

"Everything all right?" Sam asked, standing in the open doorway. He had walked up undetected, curious about why Paxton felt the need to interrupt the interview.

John shrugged. "I get the feeling Paxton wasn't comfortable with me talking to his wife."

"I got the same impression."

John motioned with his chin to the departing couple. "I'm going to take a wild guess and say that he wouldn't talk to you."

"Let's just say he was very guarded in what he had to say."

"You think he has something to hide?"

Sam shrugged. "It's definitely a possibility."

John rubbed a hand slowly against his chin as he contemplated Sam's words. "A quick background check should reveal if he's had any trouble with the law."

"I'm way ahead of you. I already called the request into the precinct," Sam informed him.

John nodded. "Where's Frank?"

"With Bridget Gallows."

"Still?"

"I believe so."

"I wonder how his interview is going," John murmured as he reached into his pocket for a small envelope. Walking over to the sofa, he bent down to retrieve the hairpin that had fallen from Christine Gallows's hair.

Sam watched him with a frown. "What's that?"

"DNA from the niece."

Sam looked at him with raised eyebrows. "I know she didn't leave the sample voluntarily."

John smiled slightly. "No, she didn't."

"So how did it happen to get here?"

"She accidentally knocked it out of her hair."

"And of course you didn't bother to mention the fact to her," Sam murmured in appreciation.

"Do I look like a fool?"

Sam smiled and walked farther into the room. "Was she receptive to the questioning?"

"She seemed to be."

"She wasn't reluctant to talk?"

"You mean like her husband?" John asked.

"Yeah."

John thought about the question seriously. "At first, she appeared nervous," he admitted, sealing the pin safely in the small envelope so that it wouldn't get contaminated.

"That could just be the stress from the day," Sam pointed out as he watched John's actions.

"It could be, but it was more than I would consider normal."

"Everybody reacts differently in these type of circumstances."

John inclined his head in acknowledgement. "That's true, and I can't say that she refused to cooperate. As a matter of fact, she said she would give us a copy of her guest list. It contains the names of her uncle's associates."

Sam's eyebrows rose slightly in surprise. "That's a start. Actually, it's more than I expected."

"To be honest, it's a little more than I expected also. But I'm not complaining. The list should help eliminate suspects."

"What was your impression of her?"

John walked over to the window and looked out at the grounds. He watched the systematic way the criminalists combed through the area where the body had been found while he contemplated Sam's question. "She seemed okay after she calmed down a little. She was talkative at least."

"Do you think her nervousness was due to the fact that she has something to hide?" Sam asked.

John turned to face Sam. "Possibly. There were some statements she made that didn't make sense to me."

"Like what?"

"Like the fact that she doesn't know if her uncle was involved with someone romantically."

Sam thought about that. "Maybe he wasn't the type to kiss and tell."

"And maybe she's hiding something."

"Like what?"

"Perhaps her uncle was involved with someone, and it's a person that she feels relatively close to," John suggested.

"What are you getting at? That she's not mentioning names in an effort to protect someone?" Sam asked.

"It's a possibility."

"If she was as close to her uncle as it appears, why would she want to protect someone who might be able to help in this investigation?"

John shrugged. "Maybe she doesn't think the person is a likely suspect."

"Therefore seeing no reason to involve her," Sam surmised.

"If I was making a premature guess, that would be the theory I would float."

"What about her husband? Is it possible she's trying to protect him?"

John rubbed a weary hand over his face. "I don't know. It would be a logical assumption."

Sam looked out into the hallway, noticing the couple holding hands. "Yeah, it would. It wouldn't be the first time that someone tried to cover up for a loved one."

"Ain't that the truth," John said, motioning to the open doorway. "Here comes Frank. Maybe he had some luck in getting answers."

"Let's hope so."

Frank entered the parlor, his gaze encompassing both men. "Well?"

Sam shrugged. "I struck out."

Frank frowned. "You were with Paxton, weren't you?"

"Yeah. But the guy's not very informative. He definitely has some reservations about talking to the police."

Frank tilted his head to one side slightly as he contemplated the remark. "Interesting."

"Why is that interesting?" John asked.

"Because in my conversation with Bridget Gallows, she let it slip that Paxton had some inquiries lately from the Feds."

"For what?" Sam asked.

"Insider trading."

"You're kidding," Sam exclaimed.

"Nope. Apparently his brokerage firm is in the process of being investigated, and it seems his name is connected to the mess."

"If they decide to indict, it would take an awful lot of money for legal representation," John murmured thoughtfully.

"I thought the same thing," Frank admitted.

Sam looked at both men. "I hate to say this, but this still points to the motive of greed."

"That's right," Frank agreed.

Sam shook his head in confusion. "But didn't you say that Paxton came from money?"

"He does," Frank assured him. "But somehow I don't get the impression that his family's reputation would survive a hit like this. If they used their money to try and get Paxton off the hook, their name would be tied to the scandal. It might not be something they would be willing to risk. The fall out could do too much damage to the family business."

"Therefore giving Paxton a motive," Sam said.

"A strong motive," Frank reiterated.

"Did anything else come up when you were speaking to Bridget Gallows?" John asked.

Frank shrugged. "Unfortunately, not too much. She was talking, but just barely."

"That could just be a reaction to the events of the night," Sam suggested.

"Possibly. What happened tonight was enough to send anyone into a tailspin," Frank said just as he heard the sound of approaching footsteps. He watched the proprietor of the bed-and-breakfast enter the room before looking at first John and then Sam. "This is Mary Jones, the owner of Crosswind."

"Gentlemen," she greeted, her voice low and soft.

John frowned at the familiarity of the voice. Quickly turning, he looked at the woman who stood before him. "Mary Brannigan?"

There was a moment of silence as the woman stared at him, confused by the use of her maiden name. Her eyes searched his features, until she recognized him. "Hello, John."

Chapter Five

John looked at the woman that he hadn't seen since high school. "I hadn't realized you had moved back to town."

"I came back last year," she said, her eyes roaming over his features. "You're looking good."

"Thanks, so are you," he replied, surprise still evident in his voice at the turn of events. His gaze flew to her hand. "You're married now," he guessed, trying to make the connection between the name he knew her by in high school and the name Frank had called her by.

"Widowed," she corrected.

John's eyes met hers. "I'm sorry," he said sincerely, his voice full of sympathy. He had always liked Mary, and he felt genuinely bad that she had suffered such a loss. The person that he remembered from high school was always a little reserved, a little shy, but she never had a harsh word for anybody. It was something he had respected her for. It was something that didn't exist with the girls that hung out with his crowd.

"Thanks."

He inclined his head, his eyes taking in everything about her appearance. She was slightly thinner and her hair was blonder, but otherwise she looked the same. He couldn't believe that the girl he had gone to school with and the woman who owned Crosswind were one and the same. She was the last person he expected to see. As far as he knew, she had moved to Boston with her family right after high school. He had not heard from his high school friends that she had come back to town. Thinking about it, he supposed there was no reason why he should have. People had a tendency to lose touch after a while, ties of friendship separating as if they had never existed. "You haven't changed a bit," he felt compelled to say, and it was an honest sentiment. Her appearance hadn't changed much, and by the looks of it, neither had her personality. She was still cool, composed, and reserved.

"Neither have you. I would recognize you any-where," she replied, her eyes automatically looking for and finding the small scar above his right eye. She felt a slight touch of guilt at the sight. She would never forget that she was the one who had caused the injury. That day would be forever burned in her memory, and she was instantly flooded with the recollection of what had occurred.

She had been out walking, upset at the discovery that she had to move out of town with her family. John had been out riding motorcycles with his friends. Wrapped up in her own misery, she hadn't watched where she was going. She had accidentally walked directly across his path, causing him to wipe out in an effort to avoid hitting her. The incident had landed him in the hospital, and she had never forgiven herself for causing the crash.

John looked at her, noticing that she was staring at the scar. He remembered how guilty she had felt about the accident. It had been the first time that a girl had sent him flowers by way of apology. He smiled slightly at the memory. "It doesn't hurt anymore," he assured her softly.

She blushed and quickly looked away. "Yes, well . . ." she began, her voice trailing off when she couldn't find any words to say.

Frank looked at both of them in confusion. "Do you two know each other?" he asked.

"We went to high school together," Mary said, shifting uncomfortably at the sudden turn in conversation.

Frank's eyebrows lifted at the news before he focused his attention on John. "What doesn't hurt anymore?"

John glanced at Mary, noticing the telltale signs of mortification. She seemed uncomfortable with the conversation, and he wanted to spare her any more embarrassment. "It's just an inside joke," he murmured, trying to get the discussion back to the job at hand.

Mary flashed him a look of gratitude, her lips silently forming the words, *thank you.*

"Talk about a small world," Sam murmured, totally missing the small by-play that had just taken place.

Mary smiled sadly. "It seems like a lifetime ago," she said, her composure firmly back in place. She looked at John. "I'm just sorry that we're meeting again under these circumstances."

"So am I," John replied. "How are you holding up tonight? I'm sure this whole ordeal has been somewhat of a shock."

Mary ran a hand through her hair, tousling it in the process. "It has been, but I'll be happy to answer any questions you may have."

John studied her for a moment, trying to determine if she was up to the interview. He couldn't miss the stress that was noticeable on her features. He knew she had been running around all night, ensuring that the guests being detained had everything they needed. He knew the night had taken a toll on her. But he couldn't forget the fact that a murder had taken place on her property. Daniel Gallows's fate was uppermost in his mind, it had to be, and he needed some answers that would assist with the investigation. "I do have some questions."

"Feel free to ask me anything."

He nodded slightly, relieved that she was so cooperative. He knew the situation had the potential to become awkward, their past association guaranteed that. "We appreciate your cooperation."

"I'll help in any way I can," she assured him.

"Then can you tell us how well you knew Daniel Gallows?"

"Not too well. Really my only dealings with him have been in regards to the payment for his niece's wedding. And that was strictly by phone and mail," she said.

"Have you ever met the man before today?" Sam asked.

"I knew who he was," she admitted.

"Did you have a personal relationship with him?" John asked.

"No. I had seen him at a couple of social events, but I was never personally introduced to the man," she said, turning and walking over to the small bar to pour a glass of water.

John glanced at her feet as she walked across the room, noticing the spiked heels that she wore. He remembered in high school that she had always dressed for comfort rather than fashion. The look of the shoes she wore were somewhat of a surprise. He guessed some things did change. "You're the one who found Christine Gallows and her uncle, aren't you?"

She took a sip from the glass. "Yes."

"Were you just out walking when you stumbled across them?" Sam asked curiously, wanting to know the true reason behind her discovery.

"I was checking the property. I wasn't really anticipating encountering any problems, but it doesn't hurt to ensure that the guests are all being taken care of. In my business, customer satisfaction is everything. Most of my business comes from referrals from other guests. I can't afford to take a chance that someone is unhappy with the service they received."

"When did you realize that something was wrong?" John questioned, his gaze staying glued to her face, watching for any outward sign of unease or discomfort. The reading of body language was one of the most under-evaluated tools that law enforcement used. Most cases were solved strictly on instinct. Chances were, if you had an uneasy feeling about the behavior of someone, it usually paid to investigate the person further.

"Actually, it wasn't until I started down the small pathway that led to the bench that I knew something was wrong."

John looked at her curiously. "How did you know that something was wrong? Did you hear a scream?"

"No, it was more of a low wail. When I arrived at the bench, Daniel Gallows was already on the ground and his niece was standing over him. There was no one else in the area. At least nobody that I could see."

"Did you notice anyone outside the fence?" John asked.

She shook her head. "I looked, but I couldn't see anyone except for a few groups of tourists in the distance. And that wasn't uncommon. Ever since the night tours began to take place, the streets have been busy into the early morning hours."

"Was there anything about the groups that looked suspicious?" John asked.

She looked across at him, confusion evident on her face. "I'm not quite sure what you mean by that," she admitted.

"Could you tell if anybody's attention in the group seemed fixated to this area? Sometimes criminals are their own witnesses. They can't seem to control the urge to see the results of their actions," John said.

She thought about his question for a moment before responding. "I can't say that I saw anything out of the ordinary."

John nodded. "Did anybody else come to see why Christine was so upset?"

She took another sip from her glass. "No. But in all

fairness to the other guests, the amplifiers from the band and the conversations that were taking place would have effectively drowned out the sound of her crying."

"Meaning they wouldn't notice unless they were close to where she stood," Frank surmised.

She inclined her head slightly. "Exactly."

"What about her husband?" John asked.

"Her husband?" she repeated. "What about him?"

"Where was he when all of this was taking place?"

"On the dance floor. The man spent most of the night dancing with every woman here. I don't think he would have noticed anything amiss if a bomb had gone off. He was definitely enjoying the festivities."

"Did you consider his behavior strange?" Sam asked.

She took a moment to think about the question. "Not really. Even though this was a wedding reception, there could be no mistake that it was also a business mixer. I heard more than one conversation going on about possible deals."

"I guess people will use any opportunity to talk business," Sam murmured.

"It's not unusual," she agreed.

"Is there anything else you can tell us?" John asked.

"I can't think of anything right now. But if I remember anything, I'll be happy to call you," she promised.

"We would appreciate that," Frank said.

Mary glanced to the open doorway. "Then if there's nothing else at the moment, I should be getting back to the guests to see if there's anything I can get them."

"Of course," Frank replied, watching as she left the room.

Sam sighed after she left. "It doesn't look like we're any closer to discovering who the person is that murdered Gallows."

"Not yet, but we definitely have a pretty good listing of who would have something to gain by taking the man out of the picture," John said.

"The bride's husband being the strongest candidate?" Sam suggested as he thought about the information they had been able to obtain.

"At first blush, he's the one who seems to have the most to hide. But we're not really sure of the reasoning for his reluctance to talk. If Frank is right, and the guy's being investigated by the Feds, that alone could explain his erratic behavior," John said.

"I agree with John," Frank said. "That kind of investigation would have to lead to a certain amount of paranoia with any kind of law official. Paxton's probably not thinking clearly right now. He almost certainly envisions us as the enemy even though his problems aren't with the local law."

"And if he feels that he's being singled out by the Feds unfairly, that could explain his distrust. Of course, there's also the possibility that there's some kind of connection between Gallows, Paxton, and the investigation by the Feds," John said.

Frank looked at Sam. "You already called in the request for a report on the guy, didn't you?"

"Yeah. Right after our interview ended."

"Hopefully there will be something in the report that will shed some light on this whole mess," Frank said.

"They promised that they would have it ready by late this morning."

Frank nodded. "Then we should definitely have a clearer picture on Paxton and his family. I already put in the request for the report on Christine Gallows and her mother, Bridget."

"And Mary Jones?" Sam asked.

"It's taken care of," Frank assured him before motioning to the open doorway. "It looks like the others are finishing up with the statements from the guests. Let's start to wrap things up here. It's been a long night. We can meet again at the station this afternoon."

"Sure," John agreed. "What time?"

Frank glanced at his watch. "Let's say around three. That will give everybody a chance to get some shut-eye, as well as allow time for the reports to come in on our suspects. I'll arrange for a search warrant for Gallows's house before I leave here, and send a team out this morning to begin taking the place apart. You two can meet them there later to start sorting through the evidence before coming to the station."

"Sounds good," John said, not overly concerned about not being present during the early stages of the search. He knew that whatever team was sent to Gallows's residence would do a thorough job of collecting potential evidence. Though the police department in St. Augustine wasn't on the same scale as ones located in major metropolises, he would wager that the quality of talent they employed was on par.

Frank nodded and began walking toward the open door. "Good. Then let's finish taking care of business."

Chapter Six

It was close to six in the morning when John finally let himself into his house. He ran a tired hand across his eyes as he walked into the living room, throwing his keys carelessly on the desk. He was exhausted. The hours spent at Crosswind had been long, and it looked like the day was going to become even longer.

He thought about the activity that he had just left. The criminalists were still at the crime scene searching for evidence, and a new shift of uniformed cops had been brought in to control the crowd that refused to leave. Most of the people that were hanging around were harmless, people who were just curious about the proceedings that were taking place. But nevertheless, bystanders had the ability to interfere with an investigation. They were too careless. Their interest in the events sometimes overshadowed common sense. And when the police had nothing to go on, no definite lead to follow, people's natural curiosity could be the enemy.

The interior of the house felt stifling, and John stopped by the thermostat to adjust the setting on the central air. Playing with the digital display of the control unit, he waited until he heard the air kick on before he headed into the kitchen. He desperately needed some coffee.

As he filled the glass carafe with water, he briefly debated on whether or not to try and catch some sleep before he went to Daniel Gallows's residence. But he quickly discarded the idea. He knew it would be a futile effort. Though his body cried out for rest, his mind was racing too much. He had never been able to sleep right after leaving a crime scene, the adrenaline always seemed to be pulsating through his veins. Today didn't look like it was going to be any exception.

After setting up the coffee maker, he stood by the counter and waited for the beverage to brew. His mind automatically began to go over the events that took place at Crosswind, and the major players that seemed to be implicated in the case. The field was wide open with possible suspects, the forerunner being Brad Paxton. John knew that if it turned out that Paxton was involved in the murder, it was a fair certainty that any help Christine Gallows was willing to give the police would fall by the wayside. He knew and he was pretty sure that Paxton knew, they would never be able to force her into testifying against her husband. And though she seemed willing to help back at the inn, even eager, John also knew her emotions were running high over her uncle's death. He didn't really believe that her cooperation would last if her husband turned out to be their number one suspect.

He thought about the odds of Mary Brannigan owning the bed-and-breakfast that the murder had taken place at. Seeing her standing before him had been a shock. He couldn't remember the last time he had worked on a case where he actually knew one of the people personally.

John tried to recall what Mary's interests had been back in high school, in an effort to fit together some pieces of the puzzle. Her ownership of the bed-and-breakfast automatically opened her character up for questioning. But no matter how hard he thought about her life back in high school, his mind drew a blank about what she did in her spare time. The realization was no revelation. He hadn't really known her that well. His dealings with her through their senior year in high school had been minimal. Other than a few words of greeting here and there, they had pretty much kept to themselves. With the exception of the day that she had walked directly into the path of his motorcycle.

As he recalled the day, he absently reached up to finger the scar caused by the incident, and he remembered how upset she had been. At the time, he didn't think anything of it. To him, it was a natural reaction. But when he called to mind her behavior this evening when he had been speaking to her, it suddenly dawned on him how composed she had been, how in control. Considering the fact that she had found Daniel Gallows's body, he wasn't at all sure if her behavior that evening was natural. His one past experience with her seemed to suggest otherwise. And though there was nothing glaringly unusual about her actions at the bed-and-breakfast, John never liked to leave any stone unturned. He had too much experience with the ramifications of the unexpected.

The thought occurred to him that he probably still had his old high school yearbook stored somewhere, and there was a chance that it might shed some insight about Mary's life. Trying to think where he would have stowed it, he went to look for it.

Five minutes later, John reentered the kitchen, his old high school yearbook safely at his side. He walked over to the coffeepot to pour a mug full of steaming coffee before carrying it to the kitchen table. Taking a seat, he placed his cup on the tabletop and opened the book to the middle. His eyes automatically began searching for the last names that began with the letter B.

His finger skimmed down the list of names until he found Mary's, and then traveled across the page to her photograph. He tapped the page with his index finger as he stared at her picture. His memory of her in high school was accurate. She still looked exactly the same. He stared at her photo for a moment longer before flipping through the rest of the pages in the book, searching for any group shots that she may have been included in. He stopped when he noticed that she had been a member of the Law Club.

John absently picked up his mug and took a sip of his coffee as he recalled that the club studied the different aspects of law, both civil and criminal. He had several friends that had been part of the organization, so he was a little bit familiar with what the Law Club represented. But the same friends that had been involved with the group were now practicing law. Mary wasn't, and her chosen profession didn't lend itself to that particular interest. Her involvement with the group was something he was curious about. Something that he felt was worth investigating.

He was skimming through the remainder of the pages in the book when the doorbell rang. Frowning at the intrusion, he cast a quick glance at the kitchen clock, noting the early hour. He briefly wondered who could be calling before he rose from his chair to answer the door.

John automatically glanced through the viewfinder before opening the door, somewhat surprised to find Sam on the other side. He stepped back to allow him to enter the house.

"Hi," Sam said.

"Hi," John replied, noticing that Sam had gone home to change. He was now wearing a polo shirt and khakis. As he looked at him, he couldn't help but wonder what Sam was doing here. He was amazed that Elizabeth let him leave the house so soon after getting home. John knew she liked to have Sam around in the mornings to help with the baby. "Is something wrong?"

Sam gave a short bark of laughter. "That's what I like about you. You always make everybody feel so welcome."

John shook his head slightly at the words and shut the door. "I just left you a little while ago. I didn't expect to see you until later. What's up?"

Sam ran a tired hand across the back of his neck, kneading the tense muscles. "Do you have any coffee?"

"I'm sure you didn't come all this way to get a cup of coffee."

"No, but I would kill for a cup. Do you have any ready?"

"It's in the kitchen."

Sam nodded and began walking in the general direction of the room. "You don't mind if I help myself to a cup, do you?" he asked over his shoulder, his hand already reaching for a mug as he passed a cabinet.

John's gaze followed Sam's actions and he smiled slightly. "Would it matter if I did?"

"No."

"I didn't think so," John said, walking over to the table to take a seat. He watched while Sam stirred sugar into his cup. "So, are you going to tell me what brought you here?"

Sam walked to the refrigerator to take out a carton of milk. He poured a little into his cup before answering. "The background check came back on Paxton," he said nonchalantly, as if they were discussing the weather.

"Already?"

"Yeah. The guy who did it owed me a favor, and put a rush on it," Sam replied as he took a sip from his mug.

"And?"

"And, it seems that Paxton and Gallows have a stronger connection than we thought."

"What do you mean?"

Sam leaned back against the counter as he looked at John. "Paxton was a major stockholder in an electronics firm."

"So?"

"So the stock in the firm took a hit, based on a large number of shares that Gallows sold."

John sat back in his chair, tilting it back on two legs as he considered Sam's words. "You think Paxton found out that Gallows was intending to sell and tipped off his broker?"

"That's what it looks like."

"Were you able to find out the reason Gallows wanted to sell?"

Sam shook his head slightly. "Unfortunately, no. And we can't find the trail for the money."

"What do you mean?"

"It was wired into his personal account at the bank, but then Gallows made arrangements to take it out as cash."

John finished the remainder of his coffee. "So we have no idea of what he did with it."

Sam shrugged. "Not a clue. The money was his. As long as he gave the bank an appropriate amount of notice that he was taking it out in a cash payment, nobody would have any reason to question the action."

"Except the Feds."

Sam inclined his head. "If Christine Gallows mentioned to Paxton that her uncle was about to sell a large amount of stock in a company that Paxton had a personal cash interest in, Paxton may have become nervous. Especially if he was unsure of the true motive behind the move."

"Meaning that he could have believed the company was in financial trouble," John deduced.

"Exactly. And if he talked to his brokerage firm and expressed his concern to someone there . . ." Sam said, letting the rest of the sentence trail off.

"He could have caused a chain reaction."

Sam finished his coffee and reached for the glass

carafe to refill his mug. "It would explain the investigation by the Feds into Paxton's involvement."

John held out his mug, indicating that he wanted a refill. "Have you talked to Frank about this yet?"

"Yeah, I caught him on the phone before coming over here."

"What was Frank's take on the information that came in on Paxton?"

Sam shrugged. "Pretty much the same as ours. You know what they say. If it walks like a duck and quacks like a duck . . ."

John smiled at the analogy. "It seems Paxton had a greater motive than we thought to take Gallows out of the picture."

"You got that right."

"I wonder what Christine Gallows will have to say about this discovery," John murmured.

"There's something else you should know," Sam said.

"What's that?"

"There was enough DNA on the leather strip that Henry found to identify it as the murder weapon."

John was silent for a moment as he digested the news. "What was the stain? Did he say?"

"He did actually."

"And?" John prompted when Sam didn't elaborate.

"Part of it was blood."

"Gallows's?"

"Yes."

John's eyes shot up to meet Sam's. "You said part of the stain was blood. What else showed up?"

"They're still running some tests, but the preliminary reports are showing that it's some type of lotion."

"Lotion? You mean like hand cream or sunscreen?"

"Yeah."

"We're not narrowing the field with that discovery. I'm sure the restrooms at Crosswind had hand lotion available for the guests, and a lot of people wear sunscreen if they're going to be out during the day."

"I know. I thought about that too. That particular revelation doesn't add too much to the case."

"There's something that you haven't said yet," John guessed, knowing Sam well enough to realize that he was holding something back.

"Something else showed up," Sam admitted.

"What?"

"You know the hairpin that belonged to Christine Gallows that you picked up?" Sam asked.

"What about it?"

"A tiny hair that was attached to that pin is a match to one found on the leather strip."

Chapter Seven

John's chair crashed to the ground at Sam's words. "Are you sure about that?"

"Henry's positive."

"How could it have been attached to the leather?" John asked, his mind trying to get a clearer picture of the evidence. There were only two theories that he could think of. One was that there was some kind of break in the material, something that would actually snag the hair, and the other theory was that the piece of hair had been mixed with some type of fluid evidence. If it was the second theory, the moisture from the fluid could have acted as an adhesive once it was dried.

Sam walked over to the table and pulled out a chair with his foot. Placing his cup on the table, he sat down. "The hair was stuck to the leather by what appears to be hairspray."

John's eyebrows rose at the words. This was the first time in his career that they had a suspect based on their personal grooming habits. "Some of that stuff is like glue," he acknowledged.

Sam grimaced. "Tell me about it. Elizabeth's hair doesn't move an inch if we're out on a windy day."

John smiled slightly at Sam's words. He had been with Sam and Elizabeth during a storm. Sam wasn't far off the mark with his words. Elizabeth's hair didn't move much at all. But Christine Gallows and Elizabeth McNeal were two different people. Just because Elizabeth used the stuff excessively, that didn't mean every woman did. "A good defense attorney would claim that the hair found its way to the murder weapon because Christine Gallows was in the immediate vicinity of where the body was discovered," John pointed out, knowing that the evidence of a single hair was only circumstantial.

"You think she would claim that the wind carried it?"

"Possibly. You know as well as I do that people come up with some farfetched ideas when they're forced to explain something."

"But it wasn't windy yesterday," Sam said.

John shifted on his chair. "There's almost always a breeze that blows off the ocean. The wind wouldn't have to be from a storm. A piece of hair is light. It practically has no weight. It wouldn't take much wind to carry it. A simple breath would probably do the trick."

"That would be a pretty lame explanation."

"It doesn't matter. It would be enough so that we wouldn't be able to prove beyond a shadow of a doubt that Christine Gallows touched the murder weapon with her own hands."

"The District Attorney would still get an indictment."

"An indictment, yes. A conviction, no. I don't think a jury would convict on a circumstantial case."

Sam was silent for a moment as he thought about John's words. "Probably not," he agreed.

"It could also be argued that someone else transferred the evidence to the material," John said.

"Intentionally?"

"Not necessarily. I would say that everybody in attendance at the wedding had some sort of personal contact with her that night. It would be easy enough for anyone to have had the small hair stuck on his or her own hand. Especially if they danced with her or hugged her."

"Which is a normal occurrence at these events."

"Exactly."

Sam was silent for a moment before saying, "Christine Gallows's hair being on the murder weapon does prove one thing."

John's thoughts paralleled Sam's. "Yes it does. It proves that the murderer was present at the wedding."

"That's right," Sam said, his eyes catching site of the yearbook that sat on top of the table. He reached out to move the book so that he could look at the cover. "What's this?"

"My old high school yearbook from my senior year."

"You saved it?"

John shrugged. "I did, but don't ask me why. I didn't save anything else from those years."

"What were you looking for?"

"I thought I would see if there's anything in it on Mary Brannigan."

"You mean Mary Jones," Sam said, reminding him that she now had a different last name.

John inclined his head, acknowledging his mistake. "I thought it wouldn't hurt to check it out."

"May I?" Sam asked, motioning to the book with his hand.

"Help yourself," John replied, pushing the book across the expanse of the table to Sam.

Sam pulled the book toward him, and turned it around so that it wasn't upside down. "Finding out that she was the owner of Crosswind had to be somewhat of a shock," he said offhandedly as he skimmed through the pages.

"That's an understatement."

Sam continued to look through the book until he finally found the page that held Mary's picture. He whistled softly between his teeth as he saw for himself that there was very little difference between her appearance in high school and the way she looked today. "You weren't kidding when you said that she hadn't changed."

"No, I wasn't. I would have recognized her anywhere."

"What else was she involved in during her senior year?" Sam asked curiously, knowing that the clubs or societies that a person belonged to in high school could give a certain amount of insight into their personality.

John reached for the book and turned the pages until he found her group shot. "The Law Club," he said, pointing to the picture with his index finger.

Sam frowned. "You think she wanted to be a lawyer?" he asked, reaching out to bring the book back to his side of the table.

"I have no idea. But I think it's interesting. You have to admit it's a big departure from what she's currently doing."

"True. But it doesn't mean anything. People change their mind all the time about what they want to do with their life. It's possible she was only exploring her opportunities."

"That could be," John acknowledged. "But there could also be something else there. I'd like to check it out."

"How? What are you going to do? Come right out and ask her?"

"Do you have any better ideas?"

Sam looked back at the picture. "Do you know any of these other people that were in the club? Anyone that you still keep in touch with?"

"A few."

"Why don't you ask them what she was like back then? The clubs in high school are usually a social outlet. Maybe someone that spent time with her could shed some light on her true reason for joining. Maybe they could give you some history on the woman herself. First hand accounts of her personality that wouldn't show up in a background check."

"I suppose I can call Mike Malone. He was part of that scene, and I play cards with him once a month."

Sam glanced at the calendar that hung on the kitchen wall. "When's your next card game?"

"Unfortunately, not for a while."

"Would Malone be receptive to questioning?"

"I don't see why not. I'm not questioning his activities. Usually people only get nervous when they think the investigation is revolving around them."

"Not always. A lot of people wouldn't want to talk to you about what took place back then. They might feel that it was a betrayal of a confidence. Especially if they were close to the person."

John shrugged off the words. "Malone's not like that. He likes to talk. It really doesn't matter what the topic is."

"Then there's no harm in asking him."

"None that I can see."

"So when are you going to call him?"

John glanced at the watch strapped to his wrist. "It's too early right now. He likes to hit the clubs at night. He's probably not even up yet."

"Maybe you shouldn't actually call him. Maybe it would be better to see him in person."

"Yeah, it might at that," John said, knowing that you could tell a lot about whether a person was being honest, just by watching their facial expression.

"Not that I'm suggesting that he would be untruthful in what he was willing to tell you," Sam said.

"Of course not. We both have enough experience with people to know that intentionally or unintentionally, they have the ability to shade the truth."

"So, you'll talk to him today?"

"Yeah. I'll head over to his place before going to the station later this afternoon. He owns a small restaurant down in the historic district. He has a manager to handle the business aspect of it, but I'm pretty sure that he usually stops in every afternoon to check on the place."

"I imagine with the amount of traffic that the area gets that he would want to keep a close tab on the books."

"I know I would," John agreed. "If we take separate cars to Daniel Gallows's house, I can head over to talk to Mike after the search winds down, and you can stay and tie up any loose ends. We can meet back at the station this afternoon."

"Sounds good."

"What time did you want to head over to Gallows's?"

Sam glanced at his watch. "How about eleven thirty? That will give me a chance to watch the baby this morning while Elizabeth goes grocery shopping. Hopefully, he'll sleep and I'll be able to catch some shut-eye myself."

John smiled at Sam's words. "I'm surprised that she let you out of the house this morning. Especially after you were gone all night."

Sam looked sheepish. "I'm sure if she was awake when I got home, she wouldn't have."

"That would explain why you came over here for your coffee. There was probably none in your house."

Sam grimaced. "Just some left over from last night. And mud was never my beverage of choice."

John grunted. "Mine either."

Sam rose from the table. "So, I'll see you at eleven thirty?"

"You got it."

"Call me on the cell if you need to talk to me," Sam said as he began walking to the door.

"I will," John assured him.

Chapter Eight

It was 11:29 when John parked his car on the long, circular driveway of Daniel Gallows's house. Several patrol cars and investigative vans were on site, and he sat in the car for a moment, watching as people filed in and out of the double entry doors, their hands filled with bags and boxes containing evidence. The amount of paraphernalia leaving the residence didn't surprise him. He knew all too well the importance of a thorough search. Items that looked to be of no consequence in the beginning of an investigation could always come back to haunt you later. That fact couldn't be ignored. He knew that you had to cover all the bases from the onset, so that there would be no room for doubt.

He glanced around the great expanse of the yard, noting the massive palm trees that were strategically placed in clusters around the property. Their bold, green fronds stood out prominently in the late morning sun, the thick brown trunks a sharp contrast to the

63

white painted house that stood in the distance. John looked at the structure. It was immense, there was no other word for it. Ornate columns framed a front porch that would put any southern plantation to shame, and the grounds were manicured and opulent. There was no mistaking Daniel Gallows's wealth when you looked at the property. Which meant that there could be no mistake that his wealth might have been the motive for his death.

As he glanced around, he caught sight of Sam standing by the CSI van, talking to one of the investigators. He was only slightly surprised by Sam's attire. He was dressed in a three-piece suit. Opening his car door, John stepped out into the blazing Florida sun and made his way over to where he stood. "Hey," he greeted as he neared the two men.

Sam turned at the sound of his voice. "Hi."

"What time did you arrive?"

"About five minutes ago."

John nodded and motioned with his head to Sam's clothing. "Aren't you hot? It's hovering near a hundred degrees outside."

Sam absently adjusted his tie. "Nope, I'm comfortable," he assured him, noticing the slight redness of John's eyes, the look of fatigue on his face. "Did you manage to get any sleep?"

"A few hours. You?"

"About the same."

John gestured to the house. "Do you know how it's going in there?"

"Pretty good from my understanding. They did a good job of securing the residence. The few servants that live in were quickly escorted off the premises, and nobody's been able to step foot inside to tamper with anything."

"Do we know where the niece is?"

"She stayed at a hotel last night."

"Does she have her own place? Or was she living with her uncle?" John asked curiously.

"She was living here with her mother. Her and her husband are having their own house built, but it's not ready yet," Sam replied.

"How did they react to being kept off the property?"

"They didn't complain. They seem to want to co-operate with us. And that always works in our favor."

"Then we won't need to worry about the family interfering with the search," John said.

"Doesn't look like it."

"Good. Then why don't we go and see what we're dealing with," John suggested, turning to lead the way into the residence.

Sam followed him inside, stopping as they entered the living room. He looked around curiously, his eyes taking in the expensive paintings that hung on the wall, the high priced artifacts around the room. "I know this stuff is expensive, but personally, it's not my style."

"Mine either," John replied absently, preoccupied with the movements of the search team. He wasn't concerned with Daniel Gallows's artistic sense. He was more concerned with whatever they would find within the confines of the house. Seeing a small group of people coming out of an adjoining room, he started walking in their direction. "Let's go see what they found."

The room adjacent to the living room was small,

but the purpose was obvious. It was an office. A heavy mahogany desk took up one side wall, with filing cabinets anchoring both sides of it. At the moment, the filing drawers were being taken apart as the files were transferred into heavy cardboard boxes.

"What do we have?" John asked, reaching for a pair of latex gloves so he wouldn't contaminate any evidence.

"Looks like business documents," one of the officers replied, not pausing as he went about moving the manila folders to their new storage space.

John started to sort through the documents. There were folders on Daniel Gallows's real estate ventures, his bank accounts, and his personal legal documents. He reached for the folder that said INSURANCE.

"What are you looking at?" Sam asked.

"A copy of the guy's insurance policies."

"Anything interesting?"

"It depends on your point of view. It looks like Christine Gallows was sole beneficiary," John revealed as he read through the document.

"Nothing that we didn't expect."

"No, it's not," John agreed, placing the file back into the box before removing another. "This is interesting," he murmured as his eyes scanned the contents.

Sam walked closer to where he stood. "What?"

"This information is on Crosswind."

"Does it have anything to do with the plans for the wedding reception?"

"No. It looks like a business prospectus."

Sam donned a pair of gloves and reached for the manila file. "The man was a heavy player in the real estate market. Maybe he was thinking of investing in it," he suggested as he read the print.

"Look toward the back of the file. There's an article from when Crosswind opened," John said.

"It could be an article his niece had cut out. Crosswind hasn't been open for that long. Maybe she was thinking ahead of places to hold her wedding reception."

"Maybe," John conceded, reaching out to pick up another file. "For some reason Gallows was saving newspaper clippings on different ventures in town."

"Can you tell if they were from the business section? From all indications, the man had his hand in a lot of financial ventures. Maybe the articles are just research on things he had a stake in."

John sorted through the papers he held. "Some of them look like they might be from businesses he had a vested interest in. At least according to what his niece has said."

Sam placed the folder he was looking at back in the box. "This could all just be part of his business records."

"Yeah, maybe," John said, opening the drawers of the desk and looking at the items neatly stored. "He seemed very organized."

"I guarantee you, he didn't make his fortune by being sloppy," Sam said as he moved off to search the bookcase that rested against a wall.

"Anything over there?"

Sam was thumbing through a book. "Doesn't look like much."

John glanced up, catching sight of several officers heading up the stairs. He motioned with his head to the group. "You want to check out where they're going? Maybe they found something worthwhile."

"Sure."

Sam and John walked toward the grand staircase, listening to the conversation that was taking place at the top of the landing.

"It sounded like someone just said the word 'attic'," John murmured.

"They're probably about to search it."

"Or maybe they already did," John said as he began to climb the stairs. He paused on the second story landing, trying to determine which direction to go in.

"It sounds like they're in the attic right now," Sam remarked as he heard the sound of footsteps from above.

John glanced around, noticing an officer standing guard by an open wooden door. "It must be this way," he said, turning down the hallway to walk in the man's direction. He looked at the officer inquisitively as he approached.

The police officer didn't need to hear any words to know what John wanted. He motioned with his thumb to the staircase.

John mumbled his thanks as he took the stairs two at a time. Once he reached the attic, he stopped for a moment and looked around, trying to get his bearings. The room was dark, with the only light coming from two small windows and the flashlights that the officers were using. He let his eyes adjust to the shadows of the room before he walked over to a trunk that members of the search team were going through.

"There's no light switch around here?" John asked. One of the technicians shook his head. "There is,

but there's no light bulb in the socket. I just sent someone down to the van to see if we had a spare."

Sam looked over at John. "A deterrent to keep people out?"

"Could be," John replied. "It doesn't seem like the
room was used much. There's no central air conditioning up here anyway." He watched the search team
sort through the trunk. "What did you find?"

One of the technicians looked up at the question and
took a step back. "Take a look."

John stepped forward to peer into the trunk. Going
down on one knee, he held a flashlight in one hand,
and reached out to pick up the pair of ballet shoes that
rested on top of some clothes. "It looks like Christine's
stuff."

"The guy must have been sentimental," Sam said.

"From all indications, the man doted on her," John
said, handing the shoes to the technician standing by
his side so that they could be catalogued.

Sam looked around the expanse of the room, watching as one of the officers walked over to the light
socket, a light bulb in his hand. As soon as he screwed
the bulb into place, light filled the room. "It looks like
this room was used basically as a storage area," he
said, noting the boxes that lined one wall, the old fur-
niture stored in a corner of the room.

John followed his gaze. "Appears that way," he
mumbled as he moved over to one of the boxes. Opening the flap, he peered inside. "There's more kid stuff
in here."

Sam watched as John took an album out of the box.
"What's that?"

John didn't glance up as he looked through the

book. "It looks like it's a scrapbook of some kind. Christine's name is on the cover."

"Scrapbook? Elizabeth is into those things. What's in it?"

"It looks like places she wanted to visit someday. She has pictures cut out from brochures and magazines pasted to the pages."

Sam frowned and reached out to take the book from John. Skimming through the pages, he said, "It would take a fortune to visit all of these places."

"Well, it looks like the woman's going to have a fortune."

"Ain't that the truth," Sam said, handing the book over to be catalogued. "It's too bad we can't tell how long ago she created that book. It would be nice to know if that book's the product of a childhood dream or an adult ambition."

"That would definitely give us some insight into a possible motive."

Sam nodded and raised a hand to his perspiring forehead. "It's hot in here, isn't it?"

John glanced over at him. "Why don't you take your jacket off? You'll be more comfortable."

"I have a better idea. Why don't we head back downstairs and check on how it's going there?"

John grinned at Sam's refusal to put comfort over fashion. Glancing around the room one final time, he took a moment to peer into a few more boxes. He found some old records, tapes, and CD's. "Most of this stuff looks like it might belong to his niece," he said, pulling out a couple of tapes and reading the names of the artists.

"It would make sense if Daniel Gallows had an active part in her upbringing," Sam pointed out.

"Yeah, I know."

"Come on, let's go back downstairs."

"All right."

Sam took a deep breath once they cleared the room. "I'm glad we're out of there. I didn't expect that a place of this size wouldn't have air conditioning throughout the whole house."

John shrugged. "By all indications, the Gallows only used the attic as a storage facility."

"It's going to take forever to sort through this stuff. We definitely didn't find anything that can be labeled a smoking gun."

"We have a lot more leg work to do to get some concrete evidence," John agreed.

Sam glanced at his watch. "Why don't we make a final round of the house and check things out? Then I'll stay here and make sure everything's taken care of, and you can head over to Malone's before he leaves the restaurant."

"I would like to cover some ground on Mary's background before the day's shot," John said, knowing that the more bases they covered before people realized what they were doing, the better off they would be.

Sam glanced at his watch. "Do you think you'll make it to the station on time to meet Frank?"

"It shouldn't be a problem."

Chapter Nine

A couple of hours later, John found himself back in the historic district. Parking his car in a public lot, he walked through the crowded tourist area to Mike Malone's restaurant, passing the old cemetery and the City Gates as he maneuvered his way to St. George Street. The streets were filled to capacity with people walking on foot to different restaurants, museums, and historical sites.

He absently reached up to adjust his sunglasses against the bright sun. The heat of the afternoon was sweltering, but it didn't seem to bother the sightseers who were out in droves visiting everything from the Bridge of Lions, to the old structures that boasted of being the oldest of their kind. Quaint shops lined the footpath of the streets that offered a glimpse into a different era, and people ignored the high temperatures of the day, content to stroll along sidewalks, seeking out interesting places to visit.

As John passed the water wheel and the oldest

wooden school house, he came to the Spanish Quarter. The area was packed with people bustling in and out of the one-and-a-half acre living history museum, a reconstructed village where people reenacted the life of the early colonists, complete with period clothes. John walked among the masses, forced to stop periodically as sightseers paused with their maps of the area, trying to determine where they wanted to go next. As he waited impatiently for a group of kids to move off to the side, he was reminded of the reason he always managed to stay clear of the popular streets. He hated crowds.

He felt a sense of relief when he saw the sign to Mike Malone's restaurant up ahead, but was surprised by the amount of people waiting by the door to be seated. He had forgotten that the restaurant was a favorite of locals and tourists alike. He should have remembered. Mike was always bragging about the people that came from miles around just to eat at his establishment.

As John walked closer to the restaurant, he absently glanced through the window, trying to catch a glimpse of Mike. He had called the restaurant prior to leaving his house, to ensure that he wouldn't be making a wasted trip. The woman who had answered the phone had assured him that Mike was scheduled to be in by noon. John hoped that she was correct. Mike had a hectic schedule juggling the restaurant and his law practice. And though he had partners in both ventures, John knew the time involved in running both businesses could be excessive.

The moment he walked through the door, he was assaulted by a rush of cold air. The feeling was a welcome relief. The temperature outside was hovering in the high nineties, and there was no prediction for the summer rain that could usually be counted on to cool things off. He stood in the entryway for a moment, enjoying the coolness of the room. Reaching up, he removed his dark sunglasses, letting his eyes adjust to the dimness of the interior. He was about to walk up to the bartender to ask about Mike's whereabouts when he noticed him out of the corner of his eye, talking to a table full of teenagers. John lifted a hand, trying to get his attention. He didn't have to wait long before Mike joined his side.

"John. I heard that you called. What's up? Is there a card game coming up that I don't know about?" Mike asked.

John smiled slightly at the question. "No, but I would like to talk to you for a few moments if you could spare the time."

Mike looked at him curiously. He couldn't miss the seriousness of his tone of voice. "Sure."

"Can we go somewhere more private?"

"Of course. Let's go to my office," Mike said, turning and leading the way.

John followed Mike, looking around the restaurant with interest. "Business looks good."

"I can't complain," Mike replied as he walked up a small flight of stairs. He stopped at a wooden door and pushed it open. "Come in."

"Thanks."

Mike closed the door, effectively cutting off all the sound from the diners. "Have a seat," he said, gesturing toward a couple of chairs.

John sat down in a chair directly in front of the desk

and waited until Mike took his seat behind the desk. "I appreciate you taking the time to talk to me."

Mike shrugged. "Any time. Can I get you something? I can call downstairs and have them send something up."

"No thanks. To be honest, this isn't a social call."

"I kind of got that impression," Mike replied. "So tell me, what can I do for you?" he asked, automatically reaching out to his phone and pressing the button that would ensure that they wouldn't be interrupted.

John paused for a moment, trying to think of the best way to start the conversation. "Do you remember a woman by the name of Mary Brannigan from high school?" he finally asked, knowing that the best way to get the answers he needed was to come right out and ask.

"Mary Brannigan? Why does that name sound familiar?" Mike asked, more to himself than John. He stretched his legs out in front of him as he made himself more comfortable.

"I think because you two were in the Law Club together," John told him, trying to jog his memory.

Mike's eyebrows rose as he recalled the name. "That's right. I remember now. She was in that club. How did you remember that? You never joined the club. I distinctly recall trying to convince you to, and you refused."

John smiled slightly at the accusation in Mike's words. "It was nothing personal. I'm just not much of a joiner."

"Tell me about it," Mike grumbled.

"Could you tell me anything about Mary Brannigan?" John asked, trying to get the conversation back on track.

"Like what?"

"Anything."

Mike thought about what John was asking. "If you don't mind my asking, why are you so curious about her?"

"I guess you didn't hear about what happened last night."

Mike leaned forward in his chair, causing it to creak. Resting his elbows on the desk, he contemplated John. "If you're talking about the murder that took place last night, I can't help but be aware of it. It was all over the news this morning. I understand that it took place at the new bed-and-breakfast that opened last year. The old Pritchard place, wasn't it?"

"That's right."

"What does that have to do with Mary Brannigan?"

"She owns the place now."

Mike paused at hearing the words. "You're kidding."

"Afraid not."

"I wonder how come I hadn't heard about her moving back to town. I still keep in touch with a lot of the people we used to hang out with in high school. I'm surprised one of them didn't mention it."

"Her last name is Jones now. Maybe nobody knew," John offered by way of explanation. He didn't put too much importance on the fact that nobody knew Mary was back in town. It was rare for anybody to rekindle an old friendship after they lost touch with someone. Time and distance always seemed to create a chasm that few people crossed.

"That's true," Mike acknowledged before looking at him with interest. "Is she a suspect?"

"Of course not," John assured him, not wanting to go into details about the case. "I'm just looking for some background on the woman while we lay the groundwork for the investigation."

"Makes sense," Mike murmured. "Wasn't she the one who walked in front of your bike?" he asked, remembering the incident from long ago.

"Yeah, she was," John admitted.

"I remember her more clearly now. I wasn't with you when the accident happened, but the news was all over the school."

"I know," John said, remembering the attention he received from his classmates when he had been released from the hospital.

"I kind of felt sorry for the girl at the time. It had to be tough to have the whole high school talking about you."

"I imagine it was."

"Talk about a small world."

John smiled slightly, thinking it was ironic that Mike expressed the same sentiment that Sam had. "Yeah. Talk about a small world."

Mike leaned back in his chair, causing it to swivel slightly under his weight. "So now you're looking to see if there's any connection between Mary and the murder," he surmised accurately.

"Connection wouldn't exactly be the right word."

"What term would you use?" Mike asked.

"I wouldn't use any term. As I said, I'm just trying to get some background on the woman."

Mike nodded slightly, accepting the truth behind the

words. "I know you have to investigate every angle. I'm not trying to give you a hard time."

"So what can you tell me?"

"Not much, I'm afraid."

"Anything would be better than nothing."

"I wish I could tell you something that could be of some help, but to be honest, I really don't recall too much about her. I think that club was the only thing that we had in common. I don't believe that we shared any classes together."

"What can you tell me about the club?" John asked, not wanting to admit that Mary belonging to the club was the true reason he had sought Mike out.

"What did you want to know about it?"

"Like I said, anything that you could tell me."

"Such as?"

"How did you spend your time at the meetings that were held? What was the main purpose of the group?"

"Basically, we spent a couple of hours a week studying different aspects of the law," Mike said.

"What did that entail?"

"Everything. The legal process, evidence, proper defense strategies. It gave everybody the opportunity to see if pursuing a career in the legal profession was something they wanted to consider. From what I can remember about Mary, she was more interested in the criminal aspects of law, than the civil. But then again, so was I. I wouldn't read anything into it."

"That's it?"

"In a nutshell. Why?"

"I was just curious. You went into law and so did the others that belonged to the club, but Mary opened a bed-and-breakfast," John said.

"Yeah, well, you know as well as I do that stuff happens in life. Maybe she decided law wasn't for her."

"Maybe."

"There could be any number of reasons that would explain her involvement in the group," Mike said just as a thought occurred to him. "I can make a call if you can hang around for a few minutes. I think I know someone who might have heard something about Mary coming back to town."

"Who's that?" John asked.

"Jessica Kahn. You remember her? She was my brother's old girlfriend."

"You still keep in touch with her?"

"Not personally, no. But I play golf with her husband every so often. She won't mind my calling. As a matter of fact, she'd probably welcome the call. There's one thing she likes to do, and that's gossip. If there's any news about anyone we knew from back then, she would probably know about it."

John thought about the offer. As much as he hated giving anyone the least little bit of information to talk about, he was interested in what the woman had to say. "Go ahead. Make the call."

Mike thought he detected a note of hesitation in John's response. "Are you sure?" he asked, not wanting to overstep any bounds. He was all too familiar with the damage that could be caused to a case if the police tipped their hand.

"Yeah. Just make sure you're discreet."

"You got it," Mike said as he picked up the phone receiver. "Don't worry about a thing. I'll just tell Jessica that I read about the murder in the paper this morning and I was calling to see if she knew anything about it. I'm positive if there's any information that she finds interesting, she'll gladly share it."

John watched as Mike dialed the phone number, and then sat back in his chair while he waited for him to finish the call.

Five minutes later, Mike hung up the phone, a look of consternation on his face. "That was interesting."

"What was? You look like you just received terrible news. Exactly what did the woman say?"

"Well, she knew about Mary moving back to town. As a matter of fact, she couldn't wait to ask me if I had heard the news this morning about the murder."

"I take it she knows that Crosswind is owned by Mary."

"You guessed correctly. She thought it was terrible how many tragedies the poor girl has had in life."

John heard just one word. "Tragedies? That's an odd thing to say."

Mike leaned back in his seat. "Apparently Mary's husband died last year in a car accident. He was on his way home from work and collided head on with an oncoming car."

"That's a tough break."

"Then there's the murder that took place on Mary's property."

"I take it she was sympathetic."

"You don't know the half of it."

"So why don't you tell me," John instructed, wondering what it was that Mike was having difficulty saying.

"Did you know that Mary's father died a few years back?"

"No. With the exception of only a few people, I lost touch with everybody back in high school."

"Well he did. He committed suicide apparently, and Mary was the one who found the body."

"Suicide?" John repeated, stunned by the information. Though he hadn't known Mary or her family very well, he knew enough about the human psyche to realize that people only committed suicide out of desperation. He felt a glimmer of sympathy for Mary and her family.

"Yeah."

"Did Jessica know how he died?" John asked.

"She said she heard that the man hung himself."

Chapter Ten

Later that afternoon, John was at the police station, waiting for Sam and Frank to put in an appearance. Sitting at his desk, he picked up his cup of coffee and took a sip of the beverage as he thought about Mike's comment that Mary's father had hung himself. He was still reeling from that fact. There seemed to be too much similarity between Mary's father's death and the murder that had taken place at her establishment. He didn't think it was a coincidence. Either Mary was somehow involved in the murder or someone was setting her up. He was deep in thought, thinking of possible connections, when Sam walked into the room.

"Hey, you're here," Sam said, walking over to get his own cup of coffee. "How did it go?" he asked, throwing the question over his shoulder as he poured creamer into his mug.

"It was interesting," John acknowledged before asking, "Did anything show up at Gallows's place after I left?"

"Not anything that's going to shed any light on the investigation. Frank's still going through some of the evidence," Sam replied as he glanced at the clock that hung on the wall. "He should be here soon."

John nodded. "Good."

"So tell me, how did it go with Malone? What did you find out?" Sam asked, taking a seat at his desk

"Well, to begin with, he had a little trouble recalling Mary at first. It took a while before he remembered her."

"It's been a long time since your high school days."

John grunted. "Tell me about it."

Sam laughed. "What was he able to tell you about her?"

"Not much. They hung out with different crowds, so basically the club is the only thing that they had in common. He remembered that she expressed an interest in criminal law back then."

"That doesn't mean too much."

"No, it doesn't."

Sam took another sip of his coffee before asking, "Nothing else came out of the conversation?"

"Not from him."

"What do you mean?"

John finished his own coffee and rose to refill his cup. "He made a call while I was there to the wife of one of his golf partners."

"Why?"

"Because she went to school with us and she likes to keep in touch with everybody. He knew that if he called her, she would spill what she knew about Mary. Especially since the murder was all over the news."

"What did the woman say?"

John turned around to face Sam, leaning back against the counter as he contemplated him across the expanse of the room. "She was very informative actually. She knew that Mary was back in town and that she was a widow. She also said something that I found extremely interesting."

"What?"

"That Mary's father committed suicide. He hung himself. Apparently from what she had heard through the grapevine, Mary was the one who found the body," John told him.

"No kidding," Sam said, thinking about the implications of John's words. "That's some coincidence."

"I know. That was my thought."

"Did you call in the request for the background check on her family?"

"Yeah. I called it in from Mike's restaurant. It's just a matter of it being processed," John assured him.

Sam nodded and then motioned to the door. "Here comes Frank."

Frank walked into the room. "Sorry I'm late. I wanted to go over some of the things that were picked up from Gallows's house before we met. Why don't we go into my office? We'll have some privacy there," he said, turning and leading the way.

"Did any of the reports come in?" Sam asked.

"The preliminary background report on Mary Jones," Frank replied. He reached for the file on his desk and pushed it in the general direction of where John and Sam sat. "Take a look."

John reached for the folder and opened it. "There's not much here," he murmured as he read the report.

"No, there's not," Frank agreed. "About the only

thing there that might be worth further investigation is that the woman is adopted. And that could have absolutely no relevance to the case."

"Both the adoption records and her original birth certificate were sealed. We'll have to get a court order to release the records," John said.

Frank shrugged. "That's standard for the state of Florida. I'll get the ball rolling today for a court order. I doubt if anything's there, but I want to make sure that we cover every angle of this investigation."

Sam leaned forward in his chair. "John found out something else about Mary Jones."

Frank looked at John. "What's that?"

"I went to see a friend of mine today to see if he could tell me anything about her background. He found out that her father committed suicide. Apparently, he hung himself."

Frank was silent while he digested the news. "So we can assume that the lady knows a little bit about strangulation."

"I think that would be a safe bet. She has to know the principle of it anyway. The autopsy report on her father would give her a general idea," John said.

"If there was an autopsy report," Sam injected.

John glanced in his direction. "There had to be. I can't imagine any jurisdiction waving it in a case where the death is suspect."

"And we should be able to obtain a copy of it," Frank said.

John nodded. "I called in the request before I came here today."

"Good. That should save some time," Frank said as he leaned back in his chair. "Did Sam mention to you that we have an actual identification of the murder weapon?"

"Yeah. And I understand it contains DNA from Christine Gallows," John said.

"That's right," Frank replied.

Sam looked at Frank. "She could be responsible for the murder. She has the most to gain financially."

"She was upset when we spoke to her. Do you think her emotions were fake?" Frank asked.

"I don't think they were," John asserted. "I think regardless of whether or not she had anything to do with her uncle's death, she would have been genuinely upset. We've all been around long enough to know that a person can commit a crime and go into denial about what they did. Especially if they had a strong enough tie to the victim. The man was her uncle, and she's not denying that they were close."

"No, she's not. As a matter of fact, from what you've told me, she's going out of her way to be help-ful. But there is another possible explanation for her emotional distress. She could be a consummate ac-tress," Sam suggested.

"Meaning her distress and her willingness to be of assistance with the investigation is all an act to cover her actions," John said, thinking about his conversa-tion with the woman. He knew it was a possibility.

"Her DNA is on the murder weapon. Like I said, that's enough to get us an indictment," Sam reminded him.

"But not a conviction," Frank replied.

"Not based on what we have so far. We'll need more against her to make the case airtight," John said.

Frank inclined his head. "Agreed. We'll have to see

what else we come up with, and whether it does point in her direction. Because we can't forget about Brad Paxton. The man definitely has a motive for wanting Daniel Gallows out of the picture, and he could have easily transferred Christine's DNA to the murder weapon. And at first glance, he appears to have the strongest motive."

"That's true. His entire future is on the line. If the Feds make a strong enough case against him on the insider trading investigation, his life will, for all intents and purposes, be over," John said.

Sam glanced at John and Frank. "We can't ignore the third person in the immediate family that might have a reason to want Daniel Gallows dead. Bridget Gallows. Money is a strong motivator. If Gallows threatened to cut her off from financial support after Christine married, she may have become enraged."

"There did seem to be some bad blood there," Frank admitted, recalling the comments he had heard from the other guests at the party regarding the woman and her relationship with the deceased. "If Daniel Gallows threatened to cut her off completely, her motive could have been pure vengeance."

John's thoughts went back to the crime scene. "You mentioned that she was kind of quiet back at Crosswind."

"That's right," Frank acknowledged. "She kept her conversation minimal. To be honest, she was showing very little emotion. Either the woman was in total shock, or she has nerves of steel."

"Everybody reacts differently to these types of circumstances," John said.

"True," Frank agreed.

"But we can't lose sight of the fact that everybody is capable of murder given the right set of circumstances," John said.

Frank looked at John. "I saw the file on Crosswind that was found at Gallows's. Do you think there's a hidden meaning there? That there might be more of a connection between our victim and Mary Jones than we're led to believe?"

John shrugged. "I'm not sure. It could just be something relating to the wedding reception."

"It's possible," Frank acknowledged.

"There's also the fact that Daniel Gallows had more than a casual interest in real estate," Sam said.

John inclined his head. "That's right. I can't say with any sense of certainty that the file has anything to do with this case. I think the only thing we can conclude right now with any certainty is that this murder was definitely a well thought out plan. The murderer chose the right location and time to commit the act where it was pretty much guaranteed that we wouldn't focus our attention on just one person."

"Going on the assumption that if there are enough numbers in the mix, there might not be any resolution to the case," Frank murmured.

"Exactly," John agreed.

Sam thought about the information they had to work with. "So, the field is narrowed down to four possible suspects."

"If not more. We have to keep in mind that there's not one thing that has been mentioned so far that would pinpoint any one individual as the actual murderer beyond a shadow of a doubt," John said.

"Do you think it's possible that more than one person could be involved?" Frank asked.

"It's happened before," John replied. "But I don't see anything here to suggest it. At least not yet."

"So where do we go from here?" Sam asked.

"Tomorrow morning I'll head over to Mary's and see if I can get any answers," John said.

"Do you think she'll open up to you?" Frank asked. "I mean, I know she seemed willing to cooperate this morning, but she might begin to feel differently when you show up again."

"I'm hoping our past association will put her enough at ease to where she'll talk," John said.

"It's worth a shot," Frank said.

"Did you want me to go with you?" Sam asked.

"I think I'll have better luck on my own," John replied. "Too many people and she might get nervous. She might think we're targeting her."

"I agree," Frank said.

"So then it's settled. Tomorrow morning I'll head over there to see what I can find out, and then we'll meet back here to sort through the case."

"It looks like from here on out, it's a waiting game," Frank said.

"Yeah, but how long do we have to wait?" Sam asked.

John gave a slight smile. "For as long as it takes for the killer to show their hand."

Chapter Eleven

The following morning, John stood on the porch of Crosswind. He glanced around the property with interest, trying to find some evidence of the chaos that was present the night that Daniel Gallows's body had been found. There was none. The grounds had been cleared, leaving nothing but the memory.

He cast a quick look at his watch before ringing the doorbell, wanting to ensure himself that it wasn't too early to be making the call. Satisfied that his timing was all right, he pressed the buzzer.

He heard the sound of footsteps before he saw Mary through the paned glass. He smiled at her slightly when she opened the door, noting the shock evident in her eyes at finding him on her doorstep. "Good morning," he greeted.

"John. I didn't expect to see you."

"I wanted to talk to you a little bit more about what happened the other night. Is this a good time?"

"Of course," she assured him, regaining her composure. She stepped back a few steps to allow him to enter the house. "Come in."

"Thanks."

She closed the door behind him. "Let's go into the parlor," she invited, turning to lead the way.

John looked around with interest as they walked through the room. "You managed to get everything cleaned up."

"I had a cleaning crew come in after they released the crime scene," she told him softly.

"They did a good job. You would never be able to tell that anything had been amiss."

"I wish that was true."

"What do you mean?"

"News travels fast. You wouldn't believe the amount of cancellations I've had since the story broke about Daniel Gallows's body being discovered in my garden."

He looked at her sympathetically. "That bad?"

"That bad. I hadn't realized just how many of my guests were from word of mouth advertising. After the first phone call came in yesterday canceling their reservation, a domino effect seemed to take place. I couldn't answer the phone fast enough."

"That's a tough break. I'm sorry that happened."

"Thanks," she said softly, motioning for him to have a seat. "Why don't you make yourself comfortable and I'll go and get us some coffee."

"Don't bother on my account."

"It's no bother. I'm not functioning at my best yet. To be honest, if I don't get some more caffeine into my system, I probably won't be able to hold an intelligent conversation with you."

"If you're sure . . ."

"I am. Have a seat. I'll be right back."

John remained standing. He glanced around curiously after she left the room. Though the room was the same one he had been in the other night, it looked different somehow. He was trying to determine what had changed when he noticed a set of photographs on the fireplace mantle. He walked over to them. He had just picked up what was undoubtedly Mary's wedding picture when he heard her footsteps approach. Turning, he offered her a brief smile.

Mary motioned with her chin to the photograph that he held. "That's my husband, Kyle."

John watched as she placed the tray that she held on the oval coffee table. He noticed the slight shaking of her hands. "I'm sorry about your loss."

She smoothed her skirt and sat on the edge of the love seat. "Sometimes things happen in life that don't make sense."

"I know."

"We had only been married three years before he died. He was killed in a car accident."

John debated with himself only briefly as to whether or not to be truthful with her on what he knew of her life. Though he knew he could possibly catch her on anything that she said that didn't correlate to the story he had heard, he also knew it wouldn't be fair to take that course. If he was going to nail her on something, he wanted it to be legitimate. Not based on rumors. "I heard. That's a hard way to lose somebody," he murmured sympathetically.

She smiled slightly. "You sound as if you've been talking to Jessica Kahn."

"No. To be honest, I don't know the woman," he replied truthfully. He didn't want to tell her that Mike Malone was the one who had talked to Jessica. He didn't want to reveal any names.

"She went to school with us. You probably just never ran into her. And you should pray that you never do. Jessica's a gossip. She always has been, and she probably always will be. She was on my doorstep when I first moved back to town, and I haven't been able to get rid of her since. She's like the proverbial bad penny. She keeps showing up."

John smiled at her analogy. "Why was she on your doorstep when you came back to town?"

"I guess she was curious about why I came back."

"You should have refused to talk to her. I'm sure if you used the excuse that you were busy, she would have understood."

"Not her. If I had refused to let her in, she would have made a pest of herself. Besides, I really can't afford to alienate anyone. I was trying to start a business at the time, and you never know where the recommendations will come from."

"I guess that does kind of put you in an awkward position."

"You don't know the half of it. But enough about Jessica. Sit down and relax," she said.

John nodded, placing the photograph back on the mantle before crossing the room to take a seat directly across from her. "I appreciate you taking the time to talk. I know that after your experience the other night, the last thing you probably want to do is talk to the police."

She shrugged slightly as she poured the coffee. "Actually, I'm getting kind of used to it. I take it that if you heard about my husband, you also heard about my father," she said, the words a statement and not a question.

He reached out to accept the small china cup and saucer she held out to him. "Yes, I did. But I'd like to hear your side of what happened. I don't put a lot of faith in other people's interpretations."

"What did you want to know?"

"Everything."

She nodded slightly and settled back against the love seat. There was a brief pause before she began. "Well to begin, we moved back to Boston my senior year of high school. But you already knew that. The day I found out about my father's transfer, was the day I accidentally walked in front of your motorcycle."

"You were upset that day."

"I was. I didn't want to leave. I liked it here."

"Which is why you moved back," he guessed.

"Yes," she replied, no longer looking at him as she recalled the events of her father's death. "We had been back in Boston several years before things started to fall apart. I was in graduate school for my MBA."

"I remember you were in the Law Club in high school. I would have guessed that would have been the avenue you would have gone."

"For a while, that was what I wanted to do. But a few classes on torts, and some pressure from my family convinced me that I would be better suited to business. I was home for the holidays when I found my father. I had gone into his office to ask if I could borrow his car. He was there, hanging from one of the beams with a noose around his neck."

John sat quietly while she talked. He noticed the tears that had come briefly to her eyes as she recalled the incident, and he had to force himself not to offer her comfort. Somehow, he got the impression that she wouldn't welcome it. It was a sentiment he could relate to. "If this is too painful for you, I'll understand."

"No. I'm fine."

"Are you sure?" he asked, not wanting to push her.

"Yes," she assured him. She took a deep breath before continuing. "Anyway, there was a long investigation regarding his death. I was positive that the autopsy report would come back and claim foul play. I mean, I never even knew that something was wrong. His business was good, at least as far as I knew."

"What do you mean?"

"My parents never talked about their personal problems with me. If there was anything wrong, I wouldn't have known about it."

"Were you close to them?"

"Exceptionally so, but they were very protective. They wouldn't have wanted me to worry."

"Most teenagers complain about overprotective parents. You don't seem to have minded," he said.

"I didn't. You see, I was adopted. And my parents made sure that I always knew how much I was wanted by them. The fact that they wanted me to have a carefree life was just one of their ways of expressing their love."

"Where's your mother now? Back in Boston?" John asked.

"No. She passed away a few years back. Heart failure."

"So you're alone now? No brothers or sisters?" he

asked, trying to remember if she had any siblings from when he knew her.

"There's no one else. That's one of the reasons I moved back here. I always loved this area, and I knew that the chances of a bed-and-breakfast being success-ful here were pretty good. At least they were. Not many people want to stay at a place where somebody was murdered."

"This will pass. As soon as there's another news story to take its place," he assured her.

"That would be true if this was anywhere else. Ex-cept this isn't the type of thing that happens in the historic district of town. This place caters to tourists. Murders are bad for business. Nobody's going to visit a town where it isn't safe to walk the streets."

"Yes they will. A lot of towns prosper regardless of the crimes that take place. Look at New Orleans. They have a high crime rate."

"But they're known for it. We aren't. Plus, as Jes-sica Kahn was quick to point out when she called me yesterday after hearing the news, there's the coinci-dence in how my father died and the way Daniel Gal-lows was murdered."

John glanced at her sharply. "She heard about the method of murder?" he asked, knowing that the infor-mation hadn't been released to the press. Keeping the information confidential wasn't uncommon. It was a ploy the police used a lot. It was a way of screening possible suspects. There was certain information that only the police would know. If it surfaced in another manner, it was usually indicative of a lead on the per-petrator.

"No. She asked how he died and I told her that from what I could tell, he was strangled."

"How did you know that?"

She shrugged slightly. "I overheard some officers talking the night of the murder. They were saying that a black strip of leather was found in one of the bushes. They thought it was going to be identified as the murder weapon."

John was silent for a moment as he digested the information. He would hate to think that one of his own inadvertently leaked the information, but if what she said was true, that was exactly what happened.

"John? Were they right? Was that the way he died?" Mary asked.

He thought about denying it, but he instinctively knew that would be a tactical error. If he was going to force the killer to reveal themselves, he would have to play the cards that were dealt. His hesitation was brief. "Yes, it was," he admitted.

"I was afraid you would say that."

"Why?"

"Because I think it's too much of a coincidence that Daniel Gallows and my father basically died the same way."

"Why do you say that?"

She became silent suddenly, as if debating an inner conflict.

"Mary?" John prompted when she didn't speak.

She looked at him beseechingly. "There's something that I need to show you."

He looked back at her curiously. "Okay."

"It's up in my room," she informed him. "Do you mind waiting for a moment? I'll go and get it."

He studied her silently for a moment. She seemed nervous all of a sudden, as if there was something she was hiding. "I can wait," he assured her.

"I'll be right back," she promised as she rose from the love seat and walked out of the room. She returned within minutes.

John glanced at the clasp envelope that she grasped in her hand, and he motioned to it. "Is that what you wanted to show me?"

"Yes," she said, walking across to his chair. She held out the envelope for him to take.

John stared into her eyes before reaching out to take it. He saw the hint of fear that she had been unable to hide, and he wondered about it. "Do you want me to open it?"

"Yes," she replied, taking a seat on the edge of the love seat while she looked at him expectantly.

John held her gaze for a moment before opening the clasp of the envelope. He reached inside to take out the contents, his eyes falling to the papers that he held. They were newspaper clippings of her father's death. "I don't understand," he said, reading through the documents.

"There's a note."

John looked inside the envelope. Sure enough, there was a small piece of paper folded inside. Pulling it out, he unfolded it. His eyes widened at the words that were glued to the piece of paper. The letters had been cut from magazines and newspapers, ensuring that nobody would be able to analyze the handwriting. He slowly scanned the document before his eyes shot up to meet hers. "When did you get this?"

"Shortly after I moved back. While I was renovating this place actually," she admitted.

"Did you call anybody about it?"

"No."

"Why?"

She shrugged helplessly. "I didn't know who to call."

John stared into her eyes, seeing the truth behind her words. "How did you get it?"

"It was slipped under the door one night while I was asleep. I found it in the morning."

He automatically glanced back at the papers that he held, his eyes reading the words once again. "This is a threat note."

"Yes. It threatened that if I opened Crosswind, history would repeat itself," she told him softly.

"Mary . . ." he began, only to be cut off by her.

"Don't you see? History did repeat itself. It wasn't a coincidence that the articles on my father's death were included with that note. Whoever left that was warning me that someone would die in the same manner as my father. And that prophecy was fulfilled with the death of Daniel Gallows."

Chapter Twelve

John looked at her. "Why didn't you mention this note the other night when you were talking to us?"

"Everything was so hectic. It was all I could do to hold it together."

"But something like this?" he asked, holding up the documents that he held in his hand. "Didn't it occur to you that you should mention this? That this was something that we would want to know?"

Mary looked at him. "To be honest, I wasn't thinking. I was in too much shock over what had happened," she told him almost apologetically.

"But Mary . . ." he said, letting the sentence trail off when he couldn't find the words to express himself.

"I'm not trying to excuse my actions, I'm just trying to explain them," she told him softly, rising from the sofa and walking over to the window. She looked outside to the garden where Daniel Gallows's body had been discovered. "After I walked up to the bench and saw Christine standing over her uncle, I didn't know what to do. But she was so upset, the only thing I could do was take control of the situation. It was an instinctive reaction. I wasn't thinking about the note I received. It was only after all the commotion had died down and everybody had left that it occurred to me that there might be a connection between the note and Daniel Gallows's death."

"Why didn't you call and let us know after you remembered it? Were you just going to pretend it didn't exist?"

"If that was the case, I wouldn't have brought it up today. I wasn't thinking clearly the other night. I don't know what else to say in my defense. I'm sorry if not mentioning this earlier jeopardizes the investigation."

John noticed her remorse and felt a surge of sympathy for her. He knew she had a lot on her plate. He didn't want to make her feel guilty over what could have actually been an honest oversight. What she claimed was true. Crosswind was hectic the night of the murder. He couldn't very well blame her because her attention was diverted. He took a deep breath and tried to put everything back into perspective. "It doesn't jeopardize anything," he assured her. "It just would have been nice to know about it earlier."

She nodded slightly in agreement. "If I could turn back the clock, I would."

John didn't respond to her words. He stared at her for a moment, thinking about what she had said. "Let me ask you something."

"What?"

"When you mentioned that you took control of the situation, exactly what do you mean by that?"

"Just that. Christine Gallows was for all intents and

purposes out of it when I walked up to her and her uncle. I honestly don't think she could have told me what day it was," she said.

"Did she notice you when you first got there?" he asked, wondering if Christine Gallows's distress could have been an act. He hated to contemplate that the woman could be capable of that type of callousness, but he knew that it was a distinct possibility. And Mary was the only person who would be able to shed some light on what the woman's true behavior was that night.

"I don't think so. She was wailing uncontrollably, like an animal in pain. I couldn't get her to answer me when I asked her what had happened. I wasn't sure if she had been with her uncle when he collapsed, or if she had found him already on the ground. When I first saw them, I thought Daniel Gallows was still alive. It never occurred to me that he was dead."

"When did you realize?" John asked, listening intently to her words as he put together the mental picture of what had actually transpired the night Daniel Gallows had been murdered.

"When I couldn't detect his pulse."

"What exactly did you think when you saw Daniel Gallows on the ground? What went through your mind?"

"Like I said, I presumed he was still alive. I thought the man might have had a heart attack. Weddings are hectic, and from what I knew about him, so was his lifestyle. He wasn't young. I just naturally assumed that was what happened. At the time, there was nothing obvious that suggested foul play."

John lifted the note. "The message on this note didn't even cross your mind when you saw him?"

"No. I thought the note was a joke when I first got it. A cruel joke, but just a joke. I didn't take it seriously."

"Yet you kept it."

"I know. I don't really know what made me hold onto it."

"Maybe subconsciously you knew that the threat behind the words was real," he suggested.

"Maybe," she conceded. "But when I received that," she said, motioning with her chin to the document that John held, "I tried to think of who I knew that would be cruel enough to send it. Who I knew that would be ruthless enough to carry out the threat. I couldn't think of anybody. So I just ignored it. Looking at the situation now, that was a huge mistake."

"What about someone you knew in Boston? Someone who may have known your father? Could you think of any of your father's associates who may have been capable of sending this?"

Mary left her place by the window and came back to where John stood. She reached out to take the papers from his hand, and looked down at them. "I can't make any connections with anybody I knew back in Boston and this. I think I mentioned to you that my parents were very closemouthed about my father's business dealings. If there was someone who had a problem with him, I wasn't aware of it."

"Those newspaper clippings are from a Boston paper," he pointed out.

"I realize that."

"Are you sure that foul play wasn't involved with

your father's death? Was it ruled out entirely?" John asked.

"As much as possible. There was no poison in his system, and they couldn't detect any heart trouble. There were no gun or knife wounds. The autopsy report stated that he died from suffocation. Nothing else was listed that was suspect. And there were no plastic bags or anything else that would suggest that someone else restricted his flow of oxygen."

"Was your father alone in the house at the time of his death?"

"As far as I know. I was at a neighbor's house, and my mother was at the grocery store. My father hadn't mentioned anything at breakfast about any company coming."

"You didn't see any cars in front of the house? There were no neighbors that would have stopped by to visit?" he asked.

"I didn't see any cars in front of the house when I came home, but I was in my neighbor's backyard. If someone had come to the house, either by car or by foot, I didn't see them."

John studied her closely, noticing her obvious distress as she relived the incident. It bothered him knowing that he was the one causing her pain, but he knew he couldn't stop the questioning. He still needed answers to questions. Steeling himself to continue, he asked, "What type of investigation was done regarding your father's death?"

She laughed slightly, but the laugh contained no humor. "Not much of one," she admitted.

"Did you or your mother push for one?"

"Yes. But since the authorities couldn't find anything that would suggest my father died of anything other than suicide, they pretty much ignored the request. The police aren't very cooperative when they believe they have a transparent case. I guess they feel that their energies would be better off spent on something that they don't consider obvious," she told him quietly, almost bitterly.

John didn't respond to her comment, he couldn't. He knew there was an element of truth to the words. He had seen too many instances when the scenario she had just described was carried out by the police. Cops were human and the police department didn't have unlimited resources. They had to set some limits on what they would and could investigate. If the authorities didn't feel that there was anything worthwhile to explore, they've been known to stonewall an investigation. John knew that first hand. "Could I ask you something?"

"Sure."

"Not to change the subject, but did you ever have any doubt that your husband's accident was just an accident?" he asked, wanting to find out as much on her background as possible.

"No, I never had any doubts. The person who hit him was a seventeen-year-old who had been speeding in a brand new car his father had given him for his birthday. His car jumped the median when he hit Kyle head on. He survived. Kyle didn't. There was never any question that the accident could have been prevented if the kid had been a little bit more responsible, but there was no doubt that it wasn't intentional."

John noticed the brightness of her eyes shimmering with unshed tears. He could tell that she was still raw with emotion regarding her husband's death. "I didn't mean to bring back bad memories."

She took a deep breath while she gained control of her emotions. "Don't worry. You didn't. I came to terms with everything a long time ago. I had to."

He nodded slightly in understanding, not wanting to challenge her statement. He knew she was trying to convince herself as well as him of the truth behind her words. He reached out for the papers that she held. "Would you mind if I took these with me?"

She handed over the documents. "No, I don't mind. Could I ask what you want them for?"

"I'll have the lab run some tests. We'll see if there are any fingerprints on them that don't belong to either you or me."

"You could do that?"

"Yes. But I'll need you to come down to the station so that we can get a copy of your prints. Would you mind?"

"Of course not."

"Good. If you can come down sometime today, it would be helpful," he told her as he placed the documents that he held back into the clasp envelope.

"I can do that."

John nodded and sealed the envelope shut. "Just out of curiosity, did you ever show these papers to anybody else?"

"No."

"Positive?"

"They never left my possession," she assured him. "Until today."

"Then we should be able to pick up any stray prints."

"Do you really think that's a possibility?"

He lifted one shoulder slightly. "Honestly, I don't know. I guess that depends on how careless the person was who sent this to you. Whoever it was went to a lot of trouble to cut out the words and letters from magazines and newspapers. That gives us an idea of where their mindset was. They wanted to be sure that there would be no recognizable handwriting. That could mean that it's someone who's close to you. Someone who's afraid that you would have recognized their penmanship."

"Or someone who is afraid of eventually getting caught," she pointed out, her thought pattern following his own. "No handwriting to analyze would be one less piece of evidence against them."

"Could be. This will all come down to whether or not they were wearing some sort of protective covering on their hands at the time."

She looked doubtful. "Do you think there's a chance of that? After all the trouble they went to in preparing the note?"

"Criminals make mistakes. That's how we solve cases. If the person who sent this wasn't wearing gloves, then there's always the likelihood we'll be able to get a couple of prints."

"And then what?"

"You mean if we find anything?" he asked, trying to clarify what exactly she was asking.

"Yes. If you do happen to find a print that doesn't match mine or yours, what happens then?"

"Then we run it through a database and see if we can get a match."

"But doesn't that only work if the person has a criminal record?" she asked curiously.

"In most cases. But sometimes people's prints are on file for security or safety reasons."

Mary nodded. "Makes sense."

John paused for a moment, thinking that she was relaxed enough for him to broach the subject of the information on Crosswind that they found at Daniel Gallows's house. "There's something else I'd like to ask you."

"What's that?"

"We found a file on Crosswind at Daniel Gallows's residence. It looked like a business prospectus. I was wondering if you would know why he had it," John said, watching her closely as he made the statement.

"A file?"

"Yes. Yesterday you had made the comment that you only knew him in a casual manner. But it seems a little odd that he would have something like that on just a passing acquaintance."

Mary was quiet as she thought about John's words. "It's possible I understated my association with Daniel Gallows yesterday," she admitted.

"What do you mean?"

"Don't get me wrong. I never really had much to do with the man. But before I opened Crosswind, I received a phone call from Daniel Gallows stating he might be interested in acquiring a certain percentage of rights on my property."

"Why didn't you mention it before?"

"I honestly didn't think it was of any importance. I wasn't interested in the offer, so I never even considered it."

"Do you have any idea of why he made the offer?"

Mary lifted a shoulder in a shrug. "At the time, he claimed that he thought it would be a good investment. That he had enough capital to pour into the place to make it one of a kind, as well as financially beneficial to both of us."

"Did you believe him?" John asked.

"I did. The location of this property is prime. It's within walking distance of the entire historic district. I knew it had the potential for being a gold mine. He had to know it too. He didn't make his fortune without realizing profitable investments."

"So why wouldn't he have just bought it outright?"

"To be honest, I'm not really sure. Maybe he just wanted to see if it was something that he wanted to get involved in. You know, start out small and expand from there."

"Maybe," John acknowledged, sitting quietly while he digested the information she revealed.

"Who can say why people do what they do?"

John smiled at her words. "Yeah, I suppose that's true. I appreciate your time today."

"I want to help in any way I can," she assured him before motioning to the coffee that was now cold. "Would you like me to make a fresh pot?"

"No thanks. I should be going," he told her as he rose from his chair, the envelope held to his side.

"I'll walk you to the door."

"Thanks," he said, falling into step beside her. He turned to look at her. "Do me a favor, would you?"

"If I can."

"If you think of anything, anything at all that you think might be useful in investigating this case, give

me a call personally?" he requested, reaching into his
suit jacket for a business card. He held it out to her.

Mary took the card and looked at it. "I will."

"You can also call me if you believe someone's
harassing you," he assured her. "If you get any more
notes or any phone calls that bother you, don't keep
it to yourself. Call me. Day or night."

She looked up at him with a slight smile. "Does that
include if it's from Jessica Kahn?"

"It includes anybody and everybody."

"I'll remember that."

"Be sure that you do."

"Thanks."

John nodded. "I'll let you know if I come up with
anything on this little care package that was left for
you," he said, tapping the envelope.

"I would appreciate that."

He looked at her for a moment longer. "I'll be in
touch," he said before turning and walking away.

Chapter Thirteen

Twenty minutes later, John walked into the police station. As he headed toward the detectives' room, he heard the sound of raised voices coming from the room, and he quickened his pace to see what the commotion was about. He was surprised to find Christine Gallows and Bridget Gallows inside talking to Sam.

"Hi," John greeted as he walked into the room. His gaze encompassed all three people. He noticed the harried expression on Sam's face, the concerned expression on Christine's, and the disapproving expression of Bridget Gallows.

Sam looked at him with obvious relief. "John. It's about time you got here."

"What's going on?" John asked, curious at the tension that was vibrating through the room.

"Mrs. Gallows brought the guest list from her wedding like she promised," Sam said.

John turned to face Christine. "Thank you."

Sam shook his head at John's words. "Her mother

is arguing that we're not entitled to see it without a court order."

John nodded slightly as understanding dawned. He hadn't forgotten what Frank had said about Bridget Gallows. It appeared as if her uncooperative nature from the other night wasn't just a reaction from the stress of the evening. The notion didn't surprise him. It was pretty much what he expected. He turned to face the woman. "If you insist upon a court order, we can arrange that."

Christine quickly interrupted. "There's no reason for things to go that far. I promised you the list, and I have every intention of giving it to you. Regardless of what my mother says."

"Maybe your mother has a valid reason for us not to have it without a court order," John began, trying to pressure Bridget Gallows into talking. He wanted to know just why she was so bent against helping with the investigation of her brother-in-law.

Bridget Gallows stared at John in silence for a moment before saying, "I don't like the idea that my daughter came here without legal representation. It's nothing personal, you understand. I just want to make sure that there are no misinterpretations about what's said."

"Fair enough," John said, going over to his desk to drop off the envelope that he had brought back from Mary's. "If it will make you feel better, we'll bring the three of you in for formal questioning. You can have your attorney meet you here and we'll interview each of you individually."

"Don't bother on my account. I'll be happy to talk to you now," Christine assured him. She glanced briefly at her mother. "If my mother wants to have her attorney present, well, that's her choice."

"It's your attorney too, Christine," Bridget Gallows pointed out.

"I realize that. But what I can't get you to understand, is that I do not need legal representation. I'm perfectly capable and willing to talk on my own behalf," Christine told her.

John listened to the conversation going on between the two women, but kept his expression neutral as he walked over to the coffee maker. He got the distinct impression that Christine could hold her own against her mother. He decided to let her. He didn't want to do anything that could be labeled as coercion, anything that could be argued as intimidation in a court of law. Cases were known to be thrown out for less. He casually looked back toward them and motioned to the coffee carafe. "Can I offer either of you a cup?"

"I'd love one," Christine said gratefully.

"No problem," John said, pouring out the requested beverage.

"May I sit down?" Christine asked.

"Of course," John assured her, watching as she cast a final look at her mother before taking a seat by his desk.

John looked at Bridget Gallows pointedly. "Mrs. Gallows?"

"No, thank you," the woman replied.

"Suit yourself," John said, thinking that her voice was as stiff as her hairstyle seemed to be. Her gray hair was piled on top of her head in a style that could only be termed as one of casual elegance. But even though she was standing under a ceiling fan, there wasn't a single hair that moved in the slight breeze. He recalled the report that had come back on the identified murder weapon, and the notation about hairspray being detected on the leather. The woman was definitely a possible suspect in Daniel Gallows's murder. Wanting to see just what he could find out, he picked up Christine's coffee and took it back to his desk. "Did you want sugar or cream?" he asked after setting the cup before her.

"No, this is fine," Christine told him.

John pushed his chair back and took a seat. He looked at the little book she held in her hand. "Is that the list?"

Christine nodded and handed it to him. "Yes. I'm afraid you'll have to make a photocopy."

"No problem," John said, turning to look at Sam expectantly.

Sam rose from his desk and walked over to take the book from John. "I'll go do it right now."

"Thanks," John replied.

Bridget Gallows sighed audibly as Sam left the room. "Christine, I think this is a mistake."

Christine glanced over at her. "I'm not asking you to stay with me. You're free to go if you want."

"I'm not leaving you alone," Bridget Gallows replied.

"It's your choice," Christine said before turning to look at John. "I'm sorry about this."

"Don't worry about it. This isn't the first time that there's been a disagreement between family members, and I'm sure that it won't be the last."

She flashed him a smile of gratitude for his understanding. "How is the investigation going regarding my uncle's death?"

John leaned forward in his chair, his arms resting on his desk as he contemplated her across the expanse. "It's going okay. But I do have a few more questions for you if you don't mind."

"Of course not," she assured him just as Sam came back into the room with the copies.

"All done," Sam said as he pulled up a chair to John's desk. He handed the guest book back to Christine. "Thanks. We appreciate your cooperation in bringing this down."

"It's not a problem," she assured him. She turned back to John. "You said you had a few more questions?"

"Yes. I won't beat around the bush. We know about the investigation going on with your husband."

She nodded slightly, seemingly unsurprised by the news. "And?"

"And, we believe that your uncle might have been indirectly involved in causing the investigation against Brad. We'd like you to tell us what you know about the situation," John said.

"I can't really tell you all that much," she said.

"Anything you can tell us would be fine," John assured her.

Christine reached for the styrofoam cup and took a sip of the coffee while she thought about the best way to begin. "I don't know where to start," she admitted.

"Your uncle was selling some stock?" John prompted, trying to give her the opening she needed to begin.

She nodded. "Yes."

"And?" he asked, encouraging her to continue.

"And I mentioned it to Brad one night at dinner."

"What exactly did you say?"

She looked down at her coffee cup, her finger absently tracing the outer edge. "Just that my uncle was selling the stock. Nothing more than that, really."

John watched her actions, looking for any sign that indicated she wasn't being entirely truthful with him. "At the time, did you know that your husband held stock in the same company?"

She shook her head. "No. He never really discussed his finances with me. I had made the comment about my uncle selling off some shares when we were discussing the wedding arrangements."

"What made you mention it?" John asked, leaning back slightly, and resting his elbow on the arm of the chair. He tried to appear casual, to keep her talking. He didn't want her to feel threatened in any way.

"I don't know. It wasn't a planned discussion or anything like that. To be honest, I wasn't thinking when I said it. I generally don't discuss my uncle's business with anyone."

"Did you tell Brad why your uncle wanted to sell the stock?" Sam asked.

Christine shook her head. "No. I didn't offer him any explanation."

"Do you know why he wanted to sell?" Sam asked, wanting her to be more specific with what had happened.

"I knew that my uncle wanted to liquidate some assets. I also knew that he told me to spare no expense on the wedding. I thought that was the reason he was selling the shares. And I just naturally assumed Brad would think the same thing."

"But he didn't?" John asked.

"No," she confirmed. "He didn't. I'm not sure how everything spiraled out of control, but when Brad heard that my uncle was selling stock, he talked to his broker about his own investments. Things kind of got out of control from there."

"How did your husband and your uncle get along? Were they friendly? Did your uncle approve of your choice in husbands?" Sam asked.

"Not at first," Christine told them. "I don't think that Brad's blind ambition won him over."

"Blind ambition?" John repeated, thinking that it was a strange way for a wife to describe her husband.

"Brad is always looking for a way to make money. Sometimes, he doesn't think of the repercussions before he acts. My uncle didn't like that. He had a more logical approach to his business dealings."

"Christine, I really don't think this is an appropriate conversation to be having with the police," Bridget Gallows warned.

John and Sam looked at Christine expectantly, wondering if she was going to listen to her mother. She didn't.

Christine took another sip from her coffee. "What you have to understand is that Brad's not malicious in any way, shape, or form. It took me a while to get my uncle to realize that."

Bridget Gallows sighed audibly as her daughter disregarded her warning. "I can't stay and listen to this," she said, abruptly turning to walk out of the room, her heels clicking on the linoleum.

Christine offered John and Sam a slight smile of apology. "Sorry about that."

John waved off the apology. "Don't worry about it. You'd be amazed at what we see around here."

"I can imagine," she said.

"Did your uncle finally accept Brad?" Sam asked, trying to get the conversation back on track. He didn't want Bridget Gallows's departure to break the flow of Christine's words or her thoughts. But he was afraid that it already had. He hated to think that the woman's departure caused the effect she was after all along, to get her daughter to stop talking.

Christine looked at Sam. "Did my uncle accept Brad?" she repeated, thinking about the question seriously. "I honestly believe he did. I'm not saying that he and Brad were best friends or anything like that, but they did come to some sort of mutual acceptance. My uncle wanted me to be happy. Just as I wanted him to be happy."

"Your husband isn't going to appreciate you talking to us," Sam warned her. "Are you okay with that? Do you need someone to see you home?"

"Are you asking me if I think Brad would harm me?" she asked incredulously, her brow wrinkled in disbelief as if the thought had never crossed her mind.

"Yes," Sam admitted. "I guess that is what I'm asking."

She gave a slight laugh. "Brad would never hurt me," she assured him. "I know he's a little uptight right now, but I can't really say that I blame him. Things have been hectic with the wedding, the investigation, and now this."

"That's understandable," John said sympathetically,

not wanting her to take offense at Sam's words. He didn't want her to lose her willingness to talk to them. He wanted to get as much information from her as possible.

Christine continued. "You'll have to excuse my mother's behavior also. She's very protective."

Sam looked at her. "You don't have to apologize. Your mother's attitude isn't all that uncommon."

"No, it's not. And we honestly appreciate the co-operation you're extending us. I know it's not always easy when the rest of your family disagrees with what you're doing," John told her sincerely.

"It's not a problem," she said. "Unfortunately, I don't know what else I can tell you right now."

"That's all right. What you've told us so far has been very helpful," John replied.

"You'll keep me informed of the progress of the investigation?" she asked, seeking verbal assurance from him.

"I'll keep you informed on the progress of the in-vestigation personally," John promised.

"Thank you. And I'll call you if I can think of any-thing else that might be important," Christine replied as she rose to her feet.

Sam stood with her. "We would appreciate that."

She nodded slightly. "Then if there's nothing else, I guess I should be going. I have some other things that I need to take care of."

"Of course," Sam said. "Come on. I'll walk you out."

"Thanks," she said before looking at John. "I'll talk to you soon?"

"Count on it."

She maintained eye contact for a brief moment. "I will," she told him before turning and walking out of the room with Sam.

John sat back in his chair, watching as the two left the room. Picking up a pen, he tapped it against the edge of the desk while he waited for Sam to return. He didn't have to wait long.

"Well?" Sam asked the moment he came back.

John sighed. "If Christine Gallows is the killer, she puts on some show."

"I know. I was thinking the same thing. Her mother's a piece of work though," Sam said with a grimace.

John gave a short laugh. "That's an understatement."

"How did it go this morning?" Sam asked.

John pushed his chair slightly away from his desk so he could rest his feet on top. "Better than I expected. Mary was very cooperative."

"Oh?"

John picked up the clasp envelope. "She gave me this," he said, opening the flap of the envelope and pulling the documents out of their protective covering.

Sam frowned and walked closer to get a better look. He stood by John's shoulder as he looked at the pages he held. "When did she get that?"

"She said last year when she was in the process of renovating Crosswind. Apparently someone pushed it under the door one night."

"Why didn't she tell us about it?" Sam demanded.

"She claims she didn't mention it the other night because she had forgotten about it in all the excitement," John said.

"Do you believe her?"

"I don't know what she would have to gain by lying about it. She didn't have to show it to me at all. And unless she's the author of this work and is just trying to throw us off track, I would say that she was being honest."

"Did she say why she didn't report it to the police when she first received it?" Sam asked.

"She said she didn't take it seriously. She thought it was all a sick joke," John replied.

"If it is a joke, I'm not laughing."

"I know. But there's one thing she said that works in our favor."

"What's that?"

"She's claiming that she's the only person to have touched this document. And she promised she'd come by later to be fingerprinted. I'm going to send this to the lab to see if there are any other prints on this besides hers and mine."

"And if there are?" Sam asked.

John looked at him. "Then hopefully we'll be able to match them."

Chapter Fourteen

Later that evening, John stopped by his favorite pizza place to pick up the order he had called in from the office. He had spent most of the afternoon in meetings, and he had skipped lunch. At the moment, he was both hungry and tired. The only thing he felt like doing that evening was crashing in front of the television.

He thought about the dinner invitation from Sam's wife, Elizabeth, that he had turned down that evening, and the disappointment in her voice at his refusal. He felt guilty at not accepting her invitation. He had always liked Elizabeth, and he knew she wanted the chance to socialize. The new baby was taking up her days, and Sam had mentioned to him that she felt the desire to mingle with adults. John was sorry that he couldn't accommodate her. The events of the last couple of days were beginning to catch up with him, and he really didn't feel that he would be fit company for anybody. The only thing he wanted was to pick up his dinner and head home.

He reached for the door to the restaurant and pulled it open. He was unprepared for the impact of a woman's body running into his. His hands automatically reached out to steady her, and he looked down at her with a questioning smile. His eyes widened when he saw who it was. "Mary."

Mary's hands gripped his forearms as she tried to maintain her balance. She blushed a fiery red at seeing the person she had almost mowed down. An apology automatically formed on her lips. "John, I'm so sorry."

"Are you okay?"

"Yes," she assured him, her voice slightly breathless from the impact of running into him.

"You're not hurt, are you?" he asked, his hands still holding onto her while he assured himself that she wasn't injured. Though he had managed to keep her from barreling full steam into him, he knew that she had hit with enough force to possibly hurt herself.

"I'm fine."

"Positive?" he asked, holding back a smile as he noticed the casualness of her outfit. She was wearing shorts. It was a big departure from what he had come to consider her new image.

"Yes," she said, smiling slightly with embarrassment. "The only thing that's hurt is my dignity."

John returned the smile. He slowly released her arms and stepped back, waiting for her to do the same. "No harm done."

"I'm not usually so clumsy."

"I didn't think you were. What's the rush? Is some-

thing wrong?" he asked, his eyes automatically looking beyond her, searching for a possible explanation
for her behavior. He remembered her telling him that
people were canceling reservations left and right at
Crosswind, and he wondered if someone in the restaurant had said something to upset her.

"No, there's nothing wrong. My order won't be
ready for another fifteen minutes or so, and I just
wanted to run into the drugstore to pick up some
items. I should have been more careful and watched
where I was going."

"Like I said, no harm done."

She shifted slightly on her feet and looked toward
the door. "I guess I should be going."

"Okay," he said, moving to the side so she could
pass. "Oh, and by the way, thanks for coming down
to the station to give us a sample of your prints."

"I wasn't sure if you knew I was there. I asked to
see you, but they said you were in a meeting."

"I was. But the desk sergeant informed me of your
visit as soon as I was through," he said.

She nodded. "Did you get back any results on the
documents you took with you this morning?"

"Not yet. Hopefully by tomorrow. The lab's a little
backed up lately. They're short staffed with summer
vacations."

She smiled wryly at his comment. "Summer vacations? Isn't it always summer in Florida?"

John shrugged. "People who have kids in school
seem to take off the same time of the year that the
kids have off. I would imagine that it makes it easier
for them to go anywhere."

"I imagine it does. Well, I won't keep you," she said, not really making any move to leave.

John noticed her hesitation. "Why don't you have dinner with me?" he invited, surprising himself as much as her when the words came out of his mouth.

She looked shocked. "Dinner?"

He smiled. "Yeah. That is what you ordered, wasn't it?"

"Well, yes, but I don't want to impose. You look a little tired. The last thing you probably need right now is to entertain someone."

"I don't look at spending time with you as entertaining."

She grimaced wryly. "Thanks a lot."

John ran a tired hand across his eyes. "That didn't come out right. What I meant to say was that I would enjoy your company tonight. I thought since we both have to eat, we could go back to my place and catch up on old times."

"Didn't you hear enough about my life? I assure you that the rest of it is boring. There's nothing interesting that's worth hearing."

"I find that hard to believe."

"It's true," she insisted.

"Let me be the judge of that," he told her, glancing at his watch. "Why don't you run next door and get what you need, and I'll pay for our meals. They're holding yours under the name of Jones?"

"Yes, but I can't let you pay," she protested.

"Of course you can."

"But . . ."

"It's no big deal," he assured her.

She reached for her purse. "Let me at least give you some money."

"I won't take it," he said, looking back toward the parking lot at several carloads of teenagers that had just arrived. "Why don't you go now, so that we can be gone before that tribe gets in here."

Mary followed his gaze, her eyes widening at the group getting out of the cars and the rowdy remarks that they were making. "If you're sure," she said, hesitation still evident in her voice.

"I am."

"Okay. I'll see you in a few minutes," she promised.

"I'll be waiting."

Thirty minutes later, John pulled his car into his driveway. Getting out, he stood with one arm resting against the hood while he waited for Mary to pull her car in beside his. He smiled slightly as she opened her door and stepped out.

"You didn't have any trouble following me, did you?" he asked, knowing that he had left her at two stoplights.

"No. I had a pretty good idea of where you lived when you gave me your address," she told him, looking around his yard with interest.

He followed her gaze. "It's not much, but it's home."

"I like it," she assured him. "It's very functional, very streamlined, and very much you."

John looked around at the landscape that consisted mostly of palm trees and a few tropical plants. "I guess this is a big departure from what you're used to," he acknowledged, thinking of her elaborate gardens.

She closed her car door with her hip. "I honestly like what you've done to the place."

John reached into his car to remove their food. "Unfortunately, I can't take any credit for it. The landscape came with the property."

She looked at his house, which was really just an elaborate beach bungalow. It looked unpretentious and very much like a home. "This seems like the perfect place to relax."

"I like it," he said, turning to walk toward the front door. He glanced back once, just to ensure that she was following him.

After unlocking the door, he stepped aside so she could pass him. He noticed that she was wearing beach sandals. "You finally dressed for comfort, huh?"

"What?" she asked, turning to look at him with confusion.

He motioned to her feet. "Your shoes. You gave up the high heels."

She smiled self-consciously. "They were only for show. As long as I don't have any guests staying at Crosswind, I figure the only person I have to dress for is myself."

He returned her smile and kicked the door closed with his foot. "Sounds sensible. Come into the kitchen and I'll get us some drinks."

"Okay."

John laid the box and bag from the restaurant on the kitchen counter before he walked over to the refrigerator. Opening the door, he peered inside. "Let's see. I can offer you, beer, wine, or soda."

"Soda's fine," she said, glancing around the room with interest.

John nodded, removing two cans of soda. He closed the refrigerator door with his hip and motioned to the table. "Have a seat."

Mary didn't move. She felt uncomfortable having him wait on her. "What can I do to help?"

"There's nothing to do," he assured her as he handed her the drink. "Do you mind if we eat on paper plates?"

"Of course not."

John motioned to a chair. "Sit down. Relax."

"Are you sure there's nothing I can do to help?" she asked.

"Positive."

"Well, let me know if you change your mind," she said, finally taking a seat at the table. She watched as he walked back to the kitchen counter. "Can I ask you something?"

He looked up from taking utensils out of the drawer. "You can ask me anything you want. I don't know if I'll answer it, but you can ask," he told her, his tone of voice teasing.

She smiled at his words. "Why didn't you ever leave St. Augustine?"

"What makes you think that I didn't?"

"I just assumed. I guess I shouldn't have."

John came back to the table, and placed a plate of food before her. "I did leave. For a little while."

She nodded, wondering at the shortness of the answer. She thought she detected something in his voice, some kind of emotion that she couldn't identify, and she was suddenly reluctant to continue with her questioning. "We don't have to continue with this conversation. It's really none of my business."

"It's no secret," he assured her.

"You seem a little hesitant to talk about it."

He glanced her way, making eye contact. "I really don't mean to give that impression."

She nodded, accepting the sincerity of his words. "Then if you truly don't mind my asking, where did you go?"

John held her gaze for a moment before responding. "New York. I was an agent with the Federal Bureau of Investigation."

"FBI?" she repeated, surprised by the knowledge.

He gave a slight laugh. "You sound shocked."

"I'm sorry. It's just the last thing I expected to hear," she said, regaining her composure. "What made you come back to St. Augustine?"

John shrugged and finished bringing everything to the table. "What do they say? That life is what happens when you're busy making other plans?"

Mary looked at him curiously, and reached for a slice of pizza. "So what happened that was so unexpected?"

"A lot of things," he said offhandedly.

"You sound so mysterious," she teased, trying to lighten the mood. She sensed that he was reluctant to talk about whatever it was that had caused his life to shift gears, regardless of what he said.

"I don't mean to be."

Mary watched while he took a sip of his drink. "I've been told that I'm a good listener," she said in an effort to coax him into talking.

He glanced at her, the smile on his lips reflected in his eyes. "You've been told that, huh?"

"Yeah. I have it on good authority."

John pushed his plate away from him as he studied her across the expanse of the table. He held the can of soda between both hands, his right thumb absently stroking the wet aluminum. "I was married before."

Mary placed her slice of pizza on the plate, stunned by his words. She didn't know why. Her eyes automatically went to his left hand, searching for a wedding ring that would support his claim.

John smiled slightly, noticing the direction of her gaze. "It was a long time ago."

She nodded and reached for her soda. "So what happened?"

"She died."

Chapter Fifteen

Mary carefully placed her glass on the table and reached out to squeeze John's hand. "I sorry."

"Thanks."

"Was she sick?"

"Yes."

She stared into his eyes for a moment, sensing his discomfort with the topic. "I guess I should have quit while I was ahead."

"What do you mean?" he asked, releasing her hand. He reached for his soda and drained the contents in one swallow.

"I should have followed my initial instincts that told me you didn't want to talk about your past."

John shrugged carelessly. "Like I said, it's not a secret."

Mary watched him. "Your wife's illness. Was that why you moved back to St. Augustine?"

John rose from the table to rinse out his soda can

and to place it in the recycling bin. "Yes. I needed a change in life, and I always liked this city."

"I can understand that. Basically I did the same thing."

John looked at her. "That's right, you did. How exactly did you meet Kyle? I don't think you mentioned it the other day," he said, wanting to get off the topic of himself.

"I met Kyle through one of my father's business associates."

"You met him while your father was still alive?"

"No," she said, smiling as she recalled the day she met Kyle. "I don't know if you know this or not, but my father was the vice president of finance at a manufacturing company. Kyle was the treasurer's son. Believe it or not, I had met him at a company picnic after my father had passed away."

"Really?"

"Really. We were always receiving invitations to the company's events. It was a family oriented company, and I guess that once you're on their guest list, you're always on their guest list."

"Sounds nice," John murmured.

She grimaced. "Not really. I had no interest in going. It was my mother who had talked me into it. She still maintained several friendships that she had cultivated while my father had worked for the company and I guess she felt pressured into attending the event. She didn't want to go alone, and I didn't have the heart to tell her I wouldn't go with her."

"I'm sure she appreciated the gesture."

"I know she did. Anyway, I really thought I was going to have a miserable time. I hadn't really kept in touch with anybody at the company, so I pretty much expected to just sit around all day, watching the clock."

"Obviously that's not what happened."

"No. Kyle had been roped into attending the picnic by his father. I think his father was hoping that he would hook up with the CEO's daughter."

"And instead he hooked up with you," John deduced.

She inclined her head in acknowledgement. "That's right. I guess I must have looked as lost as he felt. We connected immediately. And six months later, we were married."

John walked over to the refrigerator and took out another soda. Popping the top, he took a sip. "Six months? That's quick."

"There was no reason to wait. We were married only three years before he had his accident."

"You moved here right after his death?"

"Not immediately. I wasn't really sure what I wanted to do with my life. I mean as much as I hate to admit it, my life pretty much revolved around Kyle. I didn't work when we were married."

"What made you decide to open Crosswind?" John asked, walking back to the table to take a seat across from her.

"Kyle and I were talking about opening a bed-and-breakfast in Vermont. We used to go up there every fall, and we kind of fell in love with the area. But after his death, Vermont held no appeal for me."

"Too many memories?" John asked sympathetically.

"Way too many."

"And Boston held no appeal?"

"Not really," she replied, absently toying with her napkin. "To be honest, I never really liked it there. I had to move there with my family when I was younger because I had no choice, but I never had any intention of staying there permanently. So after some careful thought, I decided to come back here. It seemed a good a place as any to start over."

"From what I've been able to gather about your business, it was the right move," he told her.

"I thought so. At least until now."

John stared into her eyes for a moment before glancing at the food on the table. "I think our dinner is cold," he said with an abrupt change of subject. The topic of conversation had gotten too personal, too serious. He knew he needed to get some levity into the night.

She straightened her napkin against the flatness of the tabletop and pushed her plate slightly away. "That's okay. I wasn't very hungry anyway."

He glanced at his watch. "It's early yet. Do you want to take a walk down to the beach?" he asked, trying to think of an activity that would get them back to neutral ground.

"Now?" she asked, clearly startled by the suggestion.

John smiled slightly. "Yes. Don't you ever walk on the beach at night? It's the best time. There are no crowds."

"I think you picked the wrong city to live in if you don't like crowds. The historic district is always mobbed."

"I know," he acknowledged wryly. "That's the main reason I don't live near that vicinity."

She laughed at his words. "I think I'll take a rain check on the walk," she said apologetically. "I probably should head back home and check my answering machine. Most of my calls for bookings come in before eight. Maybe I'll get lucky and someone will want to reserve a room."

"I'm sure things will turn around."

"I hope so."

He pushed his chair back from the table and stood. "Just out of curiosity, do you host a lot of weddings at Crosswind?"

"Not as many as I'd like, but business was picking up. I think the location is good and I tried to make the atmosphere as appealing as possible."

"Weddings are a big business."

"I know. I was kind of hoping to corner a little bit of the market," she admitted. "But I guess my plans will have to change, at least until the news of the murder dies down. Maybe after the case is solved, people will come back. For now, I'll just have to wait it out."

"For what's it worth, I think you handled yourself extremely well the night of the murder. I'm sure after the dust settles, word will get out about that. Grace under pressure is always an admirable quality."

"That wasn't grace. Believe me, inside I was falling apart."

"It didn't show," he assured her.

"You know what they say. Never let them see you sweat. I've been around long enough to know that people will attack any weakness. I think it's human nature," she said.

John inclined his head, agreeing with her assessment. "I think you're right."

Mary glanced at the watch strapped to her wrist. "Well, it's getting late. I guess I should be going."

He motioned to the food on the table. "Let me pack some of this up for you to take with you."

She waived aside the offer. "No, really, I couldn't."

"It'll only end up in the trash if you don't take it. Or at the very least, fed to the sea gulls. I don't eat leftovers."

"At all?" she asked, startled by the admission.

"At all."

"Well, if you're sure . . ."

"I am. Just give me a moment."

She stood, her hands gripping the back of her chair. "I would like to thank you for everything. I enjoyed the company tonight. To be honest, I needed the company tonight. My house is too quiet. I'm not used to it."

John finished wrapping everything up for her. "You have my business card. It has my cell phone number on it. If you ever feel the need to talk, feel free to give me a call. It doesn't have to be business related."

She inclined her head. "Thank you. The same goes for you."

He looked around the kitchen. "Do you have everything you need?"

"Yes."

"You're welcome to stay a little longer if you want," he offered.

"No, I should be going. You've had a long day. You could probably use some sleep."

He grimaced wryly. "I look that bad, huh?"

"I didn't mean it like that," she assured him. "But I know you've been going non-stop since Daniel Gallows was murdered."

John rubbed a weary hand across the back of his neck. "It has been a little hectic lately."

"So relax. Get some rest."

"I could suggest the same for you."

"Believe me. As soon as I get home, I'm going to run a bubble bath and soak away my troubles."

"Let me know if it works," he said.

"I'll do that," she said, picking up the packages he had pushed in her direction. "Come on. Walk me to my car."

"I'll let you know what I come up with on those documents I took from your house this morning," he promised. "Like I said earlier, I should know something hopefully by tomorrow."

"I would appreciate that. I am curious about what'll turn up. I'm just sorry that I didn't think of it the other night."

"Better late than never. If there is something there, the lab will find it. The people who work there are very good at what they do."

"So far I've been impressed with everybody I've dealt with. The CSI team the other night seemed like they really knew what they were doing."

He smiled at the admiration in her voice. "Let me guess. You watch those shows all the time on television."

She blushed slightly. "I find them very entertaining."

"So do I. But you have to remember that what's on television is just fiction," he said.

"I know," she assured him as they approached her car.

John took the car keys from her hand and unlocked the door. Holding it open, he waited until she got in. "Make sure you drive carefully."

"I will."

He nodded, pushing the lock down with his hand. "Call me if you need me."

"I will. Thanks," she said, reaching out to turn the key in the ignition. She looked at him as the engine sprung to life. "Would you like to do this again tomorrow night?" she asked suddenly.

"What? Dinner?"

"Yes. At my place, though. I'd like the chance to repay you for tonight."

"It's not necessary," he assured her.

"I'd like to."

John stared at her. He wasn't sure if having dinner with her two nights in a row was a smart move. She was an integral part of the investigation of Daniel Gallows's death, and he couldn't lose sight of that fact. But there was something about her that he was attracted to. Something he wanted to explore. His hesitation was brief. "Tomorrow sounds good," he said, rationalizing his acceptance of her invitation by acknowledging the additional time spent in her company would allow him the opportunity to get a better feel on her, a better sense on just what she was after in life. And if he was honest with himself, he wanted to find something, anything, that would totally exclude her as a possible suspect in Daniel Gallows's murder.

"Shall we say seven o'clock?" she asked.

"Seven o'clock is fine."

She smiled. "I'll see you then. Good night."

" 'Night," he returned, closing the car door and watching as she drove off into the night.

Chapter Sixteen

The following morning, John drove over to Sam's to pick him up before heading toward the police station. As he pulled up to the house, he honked his horn once to announce his presence.

Sam came out of the house immediately, a suit jacket hooked over his shoulder. He waved to John as he walked to the car, and carefully placed the jacket in the backseat before getting into the passenger seat. "Good morning."

"Morning," John said, waiting until Sam had his seat belt buckled before he pulled out of the driveway. "How was your evening?"

"Good. Elizabeth was sorry that you couldn't join us for dinner last night," Sam felt compelled to tell him.

John grimaced, hearing the slight note of accusation in the words. "Sorry about that. But I wouldn't have been very good company. I was exhausted."

"Did you manage to get any sleep?"

"A little. I found it hard to unwind."

Sam nodded in understanding. "Yeah, I figured you would. You looked wired when you left the station yesterday. It was the reason I didn't make an issue of you not coming to dinner."

John glanced over at him, debating on whether or not to tell him that he had dinner with Mary. He didn't want Sam to infer anything from it, but he also didn't want to make a big deal about it. He knew if he didn't say anything and people found out about it, they might get the wrong idea. Which was something that he didn't want. "I ran into Mary Jones last night," he finally said.

"Oh?"

"We ended up having dinner together," he admitted, deliberately leaving off that they would be meeting again that night.

"You're kidding," Sam said, clearly surprised by the announcement. "How did that happen?"

John shrugged. "I stopped by the pizza place to pick up my dinner, and she was there picking up an order. One thing led to another, and we ended up eating together. It was no big deal."

"Do you think that was wise?"

"What do you mean?"

"It might be considered a conflict of interest since we're investigating a murder that took place on her property."

"I don't consider it a conflict of interest. You're forgetting that I know her from a different time. I don't think there's anything wrong with our sharing a meal."

Sam backed off a little, hearing the edge in the words, in the tone. He held up his hands in surrender.

"Hey, I'm not suggesting anything. But I'm telling you one thing right now. If Elizabeth catches wind of this, you're the one who's going to explain the situation."

John looked at him in confusion. "Explain what?"

"How you could have had dinner with someone else when she specifically invited you to our place."

John laughed. "Deal."

Sam settled back in his seat, adjusting the seat belt so that it wasn't crushing his tie. "So how was it?"

"What? Dinner?"

"Yeah. Did you find anything to talk about?"

"You could say that."

Sam looked over at him, a frown marring his features at the evasiveness of John's answer. "Well don't keep me in suspense."

John glanced over at him. "You're really interested in what we talked about, aren't you?"

"I have to admit, inquiring minds want to know."

John grinned at his words. "We talked about her husband actually."

"Anything there that might be beneficial to the case?"

"No. He was the son of one of Mary's father's associates. They met at a company function. Just your basic boy meets girl story."

"So there are no skeletons in her closet?"

"None that are making themselves readily known, but the case is still open. It's anybody's guess as to what we'll find," John replied as he turned into the parking lot of the police station and parked the car. "Come on. Let's go find Frank."

* * *

They saw Frank the moment they walked into the police station. He was standing by the water cooler talking to a couple of uniformed officers. Not wanting to interrupt, they waved briefly to him to let him know they were there before they headed toward the detectives' room.

"What do you think that's about?" Sam asked, motioning with his head to the trio of men that were engrossed in a conversation.

John shrugged. "Who knows. It could be anything. But Frank saw us. He knows we're here. He shouldn't be that much longer. He's pretty good about not keeping people waiting."

"That's true."

As they walked into the detectives' room, John noticed a sealed envelope lying on top of his desk.

"Looks like you have a delivery," Sam said.

"Yeah," John replied absently as he took a seat. Reaching out, he picked up the envelope before tearing open the flap.

"What is it?" Sam asked.

John read the documents. "The preliminary lab report on the papers that I picked up at Mary's."

"What does it say?"

John sat back in his chair and stretched his legs out before him as he made himself comfortable. His eyes scanned the report before handing it to Sam. "Take a look," he invited.

Sam frowned at the seriousness of John's voice. Reaching out, he took the report and read it. He looked at John when he was through. "Other than your prints and Mary's, there are none listed."

"I know. Which means that the author of that note

was wearing a protective covering on their hands at the time they created it."

"Did you expect to find something else?"

"Not really," John admitted, taking the lab report back from Sam. He glanced back down at it, rereading the data it contained. "At least Mary was honest when she said that no one else had touched the note."

Sam looked at him curiously. "Did you doubt her?"

"I don't know if 'doubt' is the right word. She received this a year ago, and that's a long time. We don't know who else had any contact with this document. I know when she handed it to me originally, she had mentioned that it was up in her room. That doesn't necessarily mean that nobody else had access to it."

"That's true," Sam acknowledged, motioning to the document that was now encased in a clear plastic sleeve. "They couldn't pick up anything on the pages. No prints or stray particles that may have accidentally gotten attached to the glue around the edges of the letters. Whoever sent that to her was extremely careful."

"Too careful."

Sam glanced at him sharply. "What do you mean?"

John reached for the newspaper articles on Mary's father that had been included in with the note. The paper was brittle and had an aged yellow hue to it, but the print was definitely legible. "It bothers me that this accompanied the note. Including this in with the note," he said, holding up the articles, "was a deliberate move. Whoever left this for her had to know her family background."

"That's obvious from the newspaper articles," Sam pointed out.

"The articles are from a Boston paper. Somebody had to be keeping tabs on Mary's family. They had to know enough about her to make the assumption that she wouldn't call in the authorities as soon as she received the note. They had to know enough about her to anticipate how she was going to react," John said.

"You think the killer is somebody Mary knows? Somebody she's close to?" Sam asked.

"I don't know. There's always the possibility that there's no connection between this note and Daniel Gallows's murder."

"There's also the possibility that there is."

"If that's the case, there had to have been someone at the wedding that we can tie to her," John said.

"She didn't mention anything to you about knowing any guests when you met with her?"

"No. But it could be that whoever we're searching for is just a casual acquaintance of hers. She had mentioned that she knew Daniel Gallows from social events. It's possible that whoever our killer is, knew Mary the same way. She said she was given this letter a year ago. If anything, it could have been originally left because someone has a personal grudge with Mary."

"Someone trying to scare her?" Sam suggested.

"Exactly."

"I don't know if I buy that."

"Buy what?" Frank asked as he walked into the room.

John looked over at him. "I got the results back on the letter that was sent to Mary Jones last year."

Frank reached for the report. "Anything here?" he asked, reading through the document.

"Not much," John admitted. "They're going to do further testing to see if there's anything they can pick up on the adhesive under the letters."

"That'll take a while. It's a tedious test."

"I know. I was hoping that whoever left it was careless and we would have had some answers today," John replied.

"I'll see what I can do about rushing the test," Frank said.

"Thanks."

Frank placed the document back on John's desk. "Leaving this was a malicious act. It could have just been from someone you two went to school with who has a bone to pick with the woman."

Frank's words gave John pause. "I never thought of that."

"Thought of what?" Sam asked.

John motioned to the papers spread out on his desk. "That this was left by someone she knew from high school."

Sam frowned. "You know someone who's capable of that?"

"I do," John affirmed. "At least I know the name of someone who would be worth investigating."

"Who?" Frank asked.

"Jessica Kahn."

Sam searched his memory, trying to recall the name. He couldn't. "The name doesn't ring a bell."

John leaned back in his chair, hearing the springs creak from the force of his weight. "I told you that when I went to Mike Malone's restaurant to find out information about Mary, he called someone."

Sam nodded. "Yeah. So?"

"That woman was Jessica Kahn."

"Did she have a problem with Mary Jones back in high school?" Frank asked curiously.

"To tell you the truth, I don't know. But Mary did bring up the woman's name a couple of times when we were talking."

"In what respect?" Sam asked.

"She said that Jessica Kahn had called her the day after Daniel Gallows's body had been discovered. She made some kind of off the wall comment about the coincidence between Daniel Gallows's death and Mary's father's death."

"Maliciously?" Sam wanted to know.

John looked at him. "I don't know. At face value, that would be the term I would apply to it. When I was at Mike's place and he had placed the call to her, she seemed to give him an earful about Mary's life."

"There's always the chance that the woman just likes to gossip," Frank pointed out, his mind searching for plausible explanations to explain the behavior.

John inclined his head in agreement. "True. But it would take a pretty insensitive person to make a comment to her about her father's death. Unless they were just looking to start trouble."

Sam rose from his desk and went to the little refrigerator that stood in the corner of the room. Bending down, he removed a can of soda and popped the top. "You think she would have left the letter for Mary?"

John shrugged. "If she was jealous of Mary during high school and found out about her opening Crosswind, it might have been enough to send her over the edge. Stranger things have been known to happen. Perhaps she thought that the newspaper clippings and the letter would be enough to get Mary to leave town."

Sam took a sip of his drink. "What would she gain from it? Personal satisfaction, an inflated ego?"

Frank pulled out a chair and sat down. "You may have something here. Think about it. If your high school nemesis comes back to town, and you want to get rid of her, what would be the best way to go about that short of murder?"

"Scare her into leaving," Sam said.

"Which she obviously couldn't do," John said.

Sam took another sip of his drink. "No. But if she couldn't get her to leave, perhaps that knowledge would be enough to force her to take some sort of action."

John turned to his computer on his desk. He quickly punched in Jessica Kahn's name, wanting to see if anything came up on the woman.

Sam walked closer to John's desk, watching his actions. "Did anything come up?"

"She has no arrest record. She doesn't even have any traffic violations listed under her license number."

"That doesn't mean that your theory has no substance," Frank said. "Actually, the more I think about this, the more I'd like to investigate the woman."

John pushed himself back from his desk. "We have to remember that even if we can prove that Jessica Kahn is the one who left this note for Mary, that doesn't prove that she was involved with Daniel Gallows's murder."

"No," Frank agreed. "But it's a good place to start narrowing the field."

"I'm with Frank. We need to find out if there's anything there," Sam said.

John nodded. "We'll head over to talk to her this morning."

"Call me if the woman's not cooperative," Frank instructed.

"Why's that?" Sam asked.

Frank looked over at him. "Because I'll see if I can pull in a few favors. The officer I was talking to outside busted the assistant district attorney's son last night for disorderly conduct at a bar. I'll offer him a deal if you feel we need to pull the woman in for formal questioning."

"Sounds good," John said, glancing over at Sam. "Are you ready to go?"

"I've been ready."

John nodded. "Then let's get this over with."

Chapter Seventeen

Later that morning, John drove his car up to the condominium complex where Jessica Kahn lived. He stopped briefly at the gated guard booth to get access to the inside grounds before driving up to the building that housed her unit.

Sam peered out the windshield to the Spanish style architecture of the building. "It's kind of stark."

John followed his gaze, noticing the red tiled sloping roof, the white stucco walls. The only landscaping appeared to be the palm trees that had been laid out symmetrically on the property. "To each their own."

"Do you think the woman's home?" Sam asked, looking at the almost empty parking lot.

"There's only one way to find out," John replied, reaching for his door handle. He stepped out from the car, and rested his arm on the roof of the vehicle as he waited for Sam.

Sam opened his own door and stepped out. He looked around curiously, his eyes catching sight of the slight moving of blinds in the condo located right above from where they stood. "What unit is she in?"

"Two twenty-seven. Why?"

"I think she knows we're here."

"What makes you say that?"

Sam motioned to the window above them. "Somebody just looked down from that window. Based on the numbers on the outside wall, that should be her place."

John glanced up. The blinds were moving slightly. They weren't parted in a way that made it obvious that someone was watching from above, but the movement of the vinyl looked suspicious. "According to everybody's take on her, the woman likes to know everybody's business."

"You mean she considers it her mission in life to keep track of her neighbors' comings and goings."

"That's another way of saying it."

"The blinds just moved again. We should probably get up there and put the poor woman out of her misery."

"You're probably right. Let's go," John said, turning to lead the way up the curved staircase.

"I wonder if her husband is home."

"I guess we'll soon know, but it really doesn't matter. We still need to talk to her."

"True," Sam replied.

Once they reached the landing, the sound of footsteps could be heard on the opposite side of the door that read TWO TWENTY-SEVEN.

Sam looked at John with a wry smile. "Should we knock or just wait to see how long it takes for her to open the door on her own?"

John opened his mouth to reply when the door was suddenly pulled open to reveal a woman in a silk pant-suit.

"Jessica Kahn?" John asked.

The woman who stood before them ran a careless hand through her raven black curls and looked at John and Sam curiously. "I'm Jessica Kahn," she acknowl-edged. "Can I help you?"

John flashed his badge. "I'm Detective Delaney and this is Detective McNeal. We'd like to ask you a few questions."

"Ask me a few questions?"

"Yes. Would you mind?"

Jessica looked down the stairwell as if expecting to see someone else with them. "How did you get up here?" she asked, ignoring his question entirely. "No-body buzzed me from the guard booth to let me know you were here."

John reached inside his suit jacket to put his badge away. "They didn't need to. This is official police business."

She took a step back, clearly startled by the an-nouncement. "Police business?" she repeated.

"Yes," John replied. He motioned with his hand to the open doorway. "May we come in?"

"Come in? I don't know," she hedged, suddenly looking nervous and unsure of herself.

"We won't take up too much of your time," John promised, looking at her expectantly.

Her hand tightened on the doorknob that she held while she considered her options. "My husband isn't home."

"It's not your husband that we'd like to talk to."

"Do I need a lawyer?" she shot back.

John's eyebrows rose slightly at the question. "I wouldn't think so," he replied. "We just want to ask you some general questions. Of course if you would feel more comfortable talking to us with your attorney present, then we can arrange to meet you down at the station."

She stared at him silently for a moment. It was a full minute before she stepped back. "No. That's all right. You can come in."

John inclined his head slightly. "Thank you," he said, stepping into the room. He looked around curiously. The Spanish design of the outside of the building was continued into the room with the arched doorways and terra cotta floors. When he heard the sound of voices, he turned, expecting to see people. But it was only the television playing in the background.

"Would you like to sit down?" she asked, her voice containing just a hint of a tremor.

"Thanks," John said, walking over to take a seat on the sofa.

Sam sat down next to him.

Jessica took a seat in an overstuffed armchair directly across from them. "I have to admit, I'm a little confused by your presence here. Did something happen with my husband?"

"No," John assured her, wanting to put her mind at ease. His intention with this visit was to find answers regarding Daniel Gallows's murder. It wasn't to cause her any unnecessary distress. "Actually, the reason we're here is to talk to you about Mary Jones."

Her eyebrows rose slightly at the mention of Mary's

name. "Mary Jones? Why would you want to talk to me about her?"

"I'm sure you heard about what had happened the other night at her place," Sam said.

"You mean Daniel Gallows's murder?"

"That's right," Sam replied.

"Yes, I heard, but what does that have to do with me?" she asked, shaking her head slightly in confusion.

"We understand that you had called Mary Jones the day after the body was discovered and made a remark about the similarity between Daniel Gallows's murder and her father's," John said, studying her face as he made the comment, trying to get a reading on the woman.

She paled slightly at his words. "I had called to offer Mary my sympathy. Nothing more," she assured him.

"Did you ever send her a threatening note?" John asked bluntly, wanting to see how she would react to the direct question.

"Threatening note? Why would I do that? I admit that I made the comment to her about her father, and I'll even admit that it was a thoughtless remark, but I have never sent anybody a threatening note."

"Did you go and see Mary when she first came back to town?" Sam asked, thinking that if the woman's reaction to John's comment was any indication, she honestly didn't know about the note. She seemed genuinely surprised by the mention of it, as if she had absolutely no clue about what they were referring to.

She leaned back into her chair. "I went to see her," she admitted reluctantly.

"For any particular reason?" John pressed.

"As an offer of friendship. I didn't realize that visiting someone was against the law."

John detected the defensive tone of her voice, and he set about to reassure her on the purpose of their visit. "We're not here to make accusations."

"You could have fooled me," she said with disbelief.

John continued as if she had not spoken. "We're just trying to find some answers. Somebody had sent Mary a threatening note when she first came back to town. We're looking into the situation to determine who could have done it."

"Mary came back over a year ago," she pointed out. "Why are you looking into the matter now? Isn't it a little late?"

"It was only recently reported to us, and there might be a possible connection between the note and the murder. We would be negligent if we didn't follow up on every lead," John replied.

"Well I assure you, I didn't send Mary anything. I have better things to do with my time than write out nasty notes and mail them. If I have something to say to someone, I usually just come right out and say it," she informed him.

John looked around the spotless living room. There was no clutter. No newspapers or magazines were anywhere in sight. "Could you tell us how you heard about Mary's father's death?"

She shrugged. "I have some friends in Boston. When the news broke in the Boston papers, mentioning that the man had previously lived in St. Augustine, they called to ask me if I knew the name."

"That's it?" Sam asked. "Your friends from Boston called you?"

"That's it. There's nothing sinister about it."

"Do you have a subscription to any newspapers or magazines?" John asked.

"No. There's no need to subscribe to any. Any news that I want can be obtained directly from the internet."

"Were you a close friend of Mary's in high school?" Sam asked.

"I wouldn't say we were close. We shared a couple of classes. That was all," she said.

Sam admired her honesty if nothing else. "So why the sudden interest in rekindling an association with her? Especially if you weren't friendly in high school?"

She crossed her legs and shrugged. "I thought she might like to have someone that she could talk to. It's not always easy when you move to a new place, even if the place is somewhere that you used to live. I just wanted her to know that I was here if she needed anything. I'm sorry if she didn't appreciate the gesture."

Sam looked at her, not wanting to respond to her comment. "She never said whether she appreciated the gesture or not. We're here for our own reasons. Not based on anything Mary suggested."

"Yet you know about my remark to her."

"She's cooperating with the investigation. Nothing more," John assured her. "We would be disappointed if she wasn't entirely truthful with us."

Jessica was silent for a moment, considering his words. "I guess I can understand that. I apologize if I sounded defensive. But it's not every day you get questioned by the police."

"No, you're right on that score," John replied, reaching inside his suit jacket for a business card. "Here's my card. If you can think of anything that you think may be related to this case, please call me."

"You're leaving?"

John inclined his head. "We've taken up enough of your time. We appreciate your cooperation."

"Are you going to the memorial service this afternoon?" she asked curiously.

John's eyes narrowed. "What memorial service?"

"Daniel Gallows's."

"Where?" Sam asked.

"At the SeaSide Chapel by the Bridge of Lions. It's being held today at one o'clock."

Chapter Eighteen

A few minutes later, Sam sat in John's car, adjusting the flow of the air conditioner vent.

"This car is like an oven," Sam complained.

"It's supposed to hit close to a hundred today," John told him absently as he pushed the electronic window switch to let some of the heat escape from the vehicle. His thoughts were on Jessica Kahn's comment about the memorial service. He was curious about who would be in attendance, curious about whether or not there would be something there that would be helpful with the case.

"It feels like it exceeded the prediction."

"It's Florida and it's July. What did you expect?"

"An ocean breeze?"

"Wishful thinking."

"One can always hope. So tell me, what do you think about Jessica's comment about the memorial service today?" Sam asked, shifting slightly so that the cool air from the vent blew directly on his heated face.

"I think I'm glad we went to visit her today."

"Why do you suppose we didn't hear about the service?"

"Maybe our connections are falling down on the job," John said, only half joking.

Sam grunted. "Or maybe it's an impromptu service. The body hasn't been released by the coroner yet, and we really don't know when they'll have completed the full autopsy. This memorial might just be something that the family's doing for the friends and relatives who flew into town for the wedding. It would be a logical assumption anyway. To do something in remembrance before everybody left to go home."

"Possibly," John murmured.

"We're going to stake it out, aren't we?"

"I wouldn't miss it. It'll be interesting to see if anybody or anything stands out."

"I agree. It's too good an opportunity to pass up," Sam said.

"What do you think the chances are that Jessica sent that note to Mary?" John asked, his thoughts going back to the original reason for their visit with the woman.

"I don't think she did."

"Neither do I," John admitted. "At first, I wasn't sure. But when she made the comment about writing notes and mailing them, I pretty much knew that she wasn't the person responsible for leaving that package at Mary's house."

"I think her only sin is that she's thoughtless and likes to gossip. Unfortunately, neither of those traits makes her a murderer."

"No. It doesn't. I think the woman definitely gets a

kick out of starting trouble, but I don't think she would cross the line from being mean spirited to being cold and calculating."

"I agree," Sam said, glancing at the clock illuminated on the dashboard. "We still have time before the service. Did you want to get something to eat before we head over?"

"Sure," John replied, putting the car in gear and reversing out of the parking lot.

Shortly before one o'clock that afternoon, John and Sam arrived at the small chapel where the memorial service was being held. They parked off to the side, wanting to stay out of the line of vision, while still getting a clear view of the people that were in attendance. Several small groups stood outside on the steps, talking amongst themselves.

John stared at the mourners, noting their somber expressions, the muted colors of their clothing. "Nobody seems to be standing out."

Sam followed his gaze. "I agree. They all look respectfully subdued."

"That must be the family," John said, motioning to a black limousine pulling up to the front of the chapel. When the driver of the car opened the back door, the Gallows family stepped out of the car. John observed them quietly. All three seemed to be lost in their own thoughts. Christine consistently dabbed at her eyes with a handkerchief that she held, her husband Brad looked stoical, and her mother's attention was focused on the guests standing on the steps. John was surprised when Brad tried to take his wife's arm and she shrugged off the gesture, walking inside on her own. "Did you see that?"

"Yeah. It looks like the honeymoon is over," Sam murmured. "There definitely appears to be some tension today."

John contemplated what he had just witnessed. "You know, I never got the impression that Christine Gallows and Brad Paxton were a match made in heaven. I think their union was more of a merger of families."

"I have to admit, I agree. As protective as he appeared the night of the murder, I couldn't help but think that the protectiveness was more a product of his distrust of authorities."

"It sounds like we read the guy the same way. But regardless of how their marriage appears, we can't forget that they're married. I think if we can pin enough evidence on either one of them to get an indictment, their relationship will automatically take precedence over any help they're willing to give the police," John said.

"That's a given. And the same is probably going to hold true if it turns out that Bridget Gallows is somehow involved."

"Yeah, I know."

"Do you know what I thought was strange?" Sam asked after a moment of silence.

"What?"

"That Christine Gallows didn't take Paxton's last name."

"I didn't really think anything of it. That's not uncommon in today's day and age," John reminded him.

"No," Sam agreed, "it's not. But women usually at

least hyphenate their maiden name with their married name."

"Not necessarily. I think it depends on what they're bringing to the table when they tie the knot. If a woman already has a career established, I could see her not wanting to lose her identity."

"Christine doesn't work," Sam pointed out.

"No, but she is bringing an awful lot of money to the marriage. She's not going to relinquish her tie to the family fortune. I don't think she wants anybody to have any doubt of just who has the most invested in this marriage."

"If that's the case, you would have to wonder why the two bothered to get married in the first place," Sam said.

"You know as well as I do that people get married for different reasons. Love, companionship, and financial security are just a few."

"I know. I guess I'm just an idealist. I like to believe that every marriage is based on love."

John smiled. "I'm sure your wife Elizabeth wouldn't have you thinking any other way."

"Remind her of that the next time you hear her complain about our dry cleaning bills."

"I'll do that," John said, knowing that Elizabeth had been trying to get Sam to cut down on using the dry cleaners for his dress shirts in an effort to save some money. She claimed that the amount of money Sam spent on dry cleaning would pay for the baby's college education if it was invested properly. John really couldn't disagree with her.

"I'll hold you to that promise," Sam said, flicking an imaginary speck of lint off of his suit sleeve.

John grinned at the gesture and shook his head.

"Seriously though, we're going to have to be careful how we handle the Gallows during this investigation. It's possible with everything that's happened so far that the press and the public are going to see them as victims, rather than possible suspects," Sam said.

"Daniel Gallows is the one who's dead."

"True. But now we're dealing with his grieving niece. She just lost the man who for all intents and purposes acted as her father. The murder happened at the woman's wedding. Don't you see? If the press get wind of the fact that we're investigating the family, they're going to have a field day with ripping the authorities apart for basically attacking the woman when she just took two big emotional hits."

"I'm not really interested in playing politics with anyone. I'm not concerned with how this looks on paper. We took an oath to defend the law, and we're dealing with a family that has a lot to gain by this man's death."

Sam held out his hands in surrender. "I'm not denying that. I'm just saying we need to be careful."

John settled back in his seat. "We'll be as careful as the situation warrants."

An hour later, people started pouring out of the chapel, lingering on the steps as they said their farewells.

Sam reached up to adjust his sunglasses as he peered at the crowd. "There's the family," he said, gesturing with his chin to where they waited by the limousine. "We're following them, aren't we?"

"We'll be right behind them as soon as they leave,"

John assured him, watching as they got into the car. He waited until the limousine pulled away from the curb before he started his engine.

Pulling out of the parking lot, John made sure he kept a respectable distance between the vehicles to avoid any possible suspicion. The purpose of this venture was to get information. And he knew he wasn't going to be able to do that if he made anybody nervous.

"They're signaling a turn up ahead," Sam said.

"I caught it," John said, following the limousine. He slowed down as he noticed the black luxury car pull up to a curb.

"Any idea of where they stopped?" Sam asked, unable to get a clear view of the sign posted outside the building.

"The name outside reads Sebastian Langley, Attorney at Law."

Sam looked at John inquiringly. "Do we know when the reading of Gallows's will was?"

"No. The topic never came up. There was no reason why it would have. It has nothing to do with the investigation that's going on," John said.

"Yet."

"Yet," John agreed, shutting down his engine as he watched the trio exit the limousine.

"What I wouldn't give to be a fly on the wall."

John smirked. "I don't think the long arm of the law is going to stretch enough today to get you inside that office. Attorney-client privilege."

Sam reached out to unbuckle his seat belt, and straightened his jacket before leaning back in the seat.

"There's always a chance that this visit has something to do with Brad's legal problems."

"Possibly. It could also be that the family is just getting some legal advice on how to proceed with the investigation going on."

"Maybe. But I don't think they have any room to complain. I think we've been extremely courteous with them so far. We could've pulled both Brad Paxton and Bridget Gallows in for formal questioning just based on their behavior the night of the murder," Sam said.

"Yeah, I know. But sometimes you get more with a softer touch. The stakes didn't rise high enough yet to play hardball. I want a definitive suspect before we take things that far. I don't want there to be any wiggle room when it comes time for trial. If we don't pinpoint one individual, we're going to have a problem with the defense once this case goes to court. You know as well as I do that they'll claim reasonable doubt if we have too long a list of possible suspects."

"I realize we have to be careful, but I don't like giving these people the upper hand," Sam said.

"We have to be more than just careful. We can't afford to take any chances. This is a circumstantial case so far. One wrong step, and we'll lose any chance of a conviction," John responded.

"I guess we should count ourselves lucky that none of the suspects appear to be a flight risk. I think we have time on our side."

"I hope so."

It was only fifteen minutes before the family came back outside.

"That was quick," John said.

"Yeah, it was."

"Come on. Let's see where they're heading to," John said, following the limousine as it started to pull away.

Sam looked around curiously as they drove to a residential community on the outskirts of the historic district. The small custom built houses were set neatly back from the curb, and the lawns were well manicured. Large shaded oak trees and natural vegetation gave the area a distinct look, without being ostentatious. "I wonder who they know that lives here."

"I don't know. They're pulling into the driveway on the corner."

Sam glanced around. "Do you see a street sign anywhere? I can call the station and have them run a trace on the residence."

John squinted his eyes in an effort to read the street sign visible on the corner near where the limousine was parked. "It's Maple Drive. The actual house number looks like it's going to be 3504."

Sam reached for his cell phone and dialed the station. After a brief conversation, he disconnected the call.

"Well?" John asked.

"It looks like Bridget Gallows bought herself a house."

Chapter Nineteen

Later that afternoon, John and Sam were at their desks reviewing the report they had been able to pull on the real estate Bridget Gallows had just acquired.

"According to this, the funds used to purchase the property were transferred from Christine Gallows's personal checking account," John said as he read the data.

"The woman's not wasting any time in spending her inheritance."

"No, she's not," John murmured. "But we have to keep in mind that Christine and her husband have enough money of their own to account for that acquisition. Even before Gallows's death."

"Trust me, there's no way I can forget that. Did anything else come in on this case?" Sam asked, motioning to the files on John's desk.

John sorted through the stack of folders. "No. I was hoping we would have the final results on that letter that Mary gave us."

"Like Frank said, that's probably going to take some time," Sam said.

"Yeah, I know. But when I saw Frank earlier in the hallway, he said he was promised the rest of the information sometime this afternoon."

"Well, I hope it gets here soon. I promised Elizabeth I would make it home for dinner tonight. I'll never hear the end of it if I don't show up."

"I'm sure she'll forgive you if you're late," John said, looking over to the doorway as he heard the sound of footsteps. "Here comes Frank now."

Frank walked into the room, his shirt sleeves rolled up to his elbows and his tie loosened at his neck. "I'm glad you two are still here."

John looked at the clasp envelope Frank held in his hand. "Is that one of the reports?"

"Yeah. It just arrived. Take a look," Frank said, handing over the document.

John reached for the envelope, and undid the clasp. "What is it?"

"Read it for yourself," Frank said, reaching out with a foot to pull up a chair.

Sam frowned. "Who's the report on?"

"Mary," John replied, his eyes skimming through the document. "It's the sealed adoption record and original birth certificate."

"What does it say?" Sam asked curiously, noticing John's preoccupation with the report.

John glanced up, his eyes meeting Sam's. "Daniel Gallows is Mary Jones' biological father."

Sam was quiet for a moment as he contemplated John's words. "I never expected that."

Frank's gaze encompassed both men. "This might

explain the business prospectus we found at his residence."

"Yeah, it might," John said.

"Do you think Mary knows the connection she shares with the man?" Sam asked.

John ran a weary hand across the back of his neck. "She knows she's adopted, that much she told me. But she never mentioned if she was aware of who her biological parents were."

Frank shrugged. "This might be something that she's totally in the dark on. Something that will shock her. You know as well as I do that it's never easy getting a court order to release the records. Sealed records are for the protection of both parties, not just one."

"But if it was a private adoption, it could be that everybody involved knew each other. The sealed records might have been a formality for the public," John said.

"It's a possibility," Frank agreed.

"We have to talk to her about it. If she's aware of it, we should be able to judge it by her reaction. If she's not, she has the right to know that the man who died on her property was her biological father," Sam said.

John nodded. "Let me do it."

"Alone?" Frank asked.

"Yeah. I'll go over there after we're done here. I think it would be better if she didn't have an audience. If she's not aware of the information, it'll be a shock. And if she is aware of it, I might be able to get her to talk."

Sam thought about what they had just learned. "You

know, even if she did know about Gallows, it doesn't necessarily mean anything. I know a lot of people who are adopted that wouldn't give their birth parents the time of day. I guess they feel some sort of betrayal from them to begin with."

"I know," John said.

"You know the woman better than I do. If you think it's best that you handle this alone, I'm with you," Sam said.

"I do think that it's the best way to go about it."

"She's been pretty forthcoming with you so far, hasn't she?" Frank asked.

"She seemed to have been very cooperative," John replied.

"Then you handling this alone shouldn't be a problem. But call me on the cell after you're through. I want to know your reading on how she accepted the news," Frank said.

"I will."

A short time later, John was on his way to Mary's to talk to her about what they had discovered. He was curious about how she was going to react to the news that Daniel Gallows was her biological father.

He had no doubt that if it turned out she was hearing the news for the first time, she would be able to accept it. Her sense of self was strong, and the people who raised her did a good job of instilling that. But he also knew there was a chance that she was already aware of what was listed on her original birth certificate. It was that thought that bothered him. Because if that was the case, she couldn't be eliminated as a suspect in Daniel Gallows's murder.

The traffic slowed slightly, and John waited impatiently for it to move. As soon as he could, he changed lanes so that he could make the turn that led to Crosswind.

John decreased his speed as he approached the property, frowning when he caught sight of a sports car that he couldn't identify. He read the license plate. Curiosity had him reaching for his cell phone, and he quickly dialed the phone number to the station.

"Put me through to Sam McNeal," John demanded of the dispatcher as soon as his call was answered. He waited impatiently for Sam to pick up the phone.

Sam picked up on the second ring. "McNeal."

"It's John."

"What's up?"

"I need you to run a plate for me."

"Why? Was there an accident?" Sam asked.

"No. There's a car in front of Mary's. I want to know who it belongs to. If she has guests booked, I want to arrange to talk to her in a more private location."

"Sure. Give me a minute to get something to write with," Sam said.

John heard the sound of paper rustling in the background. "Ready?"

"Shoot."

John read off the license plate number and waited while Sam punched the information into the computer. "What does it come up as?" he asked impatiently when he could no longer hear the clacking of the keyboard.

"The car's registered to Mary Jones."

"Are you sure?" John asked, knowing that the car

sitting in her driveway wasn't the one she had been driving last night.

"That's what's coming up. Why?"

"I saw her car last night when I had dinner with her. It was a different make and model."

"Hold on a moment. Let me check something," Sam said. He came back on the line a minute later. "She has two cars registered under her name."

"That's interesting."

"But not that unusual. The woman runs a bed-and-breakfast. I'm sure two cars come in handy. Especially if she shuttles guests around."

"Yeah, I guess," John said, knowing Sam's explanation made sense. "Look, I'm pulling into her driveway now, so I'm going to go. I'll talk to you later," he promised before disconnecting the call. He threw his cell phone carelessly into the passenger seat as he drove through the wrought iron gates that surrounded her property. After parking the car, he opened the door and stepped out into the late afternoon sun. Shrugging into his suit jacket, he walked up the steps that led to the veranda.

As he stepped onto the porch, he heard the wood creak under his weight. When a floorboard shifted beneath his foot, he frowned, and crouched down to see what caused the board to become loose. Studying the planks, he ran his fingertips along the outer edge of the wood, trying to determine where the separation had occurred between the board and the frame. When he felt a weak spot, he pulled. He didn't have to apply a lot of pressure for the board to come up in his hand.

John looked into the dark abyss that had been revealed. Reaching into his suit jacket, he removed a

small penlight and positioned the light into the opening. He immediately saw something black.

At first glance, he thought it was a snake. Florida
was full of them, and he wouldn't have been surprised
if one of them had decided to make the area under
Mary's porch home. When the object didn't move,
John moved in to get a closer look. It was then that
he saw that he had actually uncovered a long piece of
black leather, identical in size to the one that had been
recovered as the murder weapon. He reached in to pull
it out, his mind grappling with the discovery.

He was staring at the piece of leather when he heard
the sound of footsteps. He glanced up to find Mary
standing in the doorway, looking at him curiously.

"John? What are you doing?"

John's eyes locked with hers. He slowly held up the
black strip of leather. "I was going to ask you the same
thing."

Mary frowned at his words, at his tone of voice.
She looked at him in confusion until her eyes caught
sight of what he held. She stared at it blankly.

"Mary? Can you explain this?" John asked, wanting
her to be able to offer a plausible explanation of why
the piece of black leather had been buried under her
porch. He thought about all the reasons she could offer. That she didn't know anything about it, that she
didn't know how it got there, or that someone else had
placed it there. He knew none of them would be the
truth. The board on the porch wasn't loose the night
of the murder, or the morning when he had come to
talk to her. He would have noticed it. Which meant
that the object had been hidden after the last time he
had been at Crosswind. His gut told him Mary had to

be responsible for the action. It was the only thing that made sense. Nobody else would have come back to the property to hide the item. There was no reason to. It wasn't the actual murder weapon. John could think of only one explanation of why someone would have hidden the leather tie. And that was guilt.

She looked at him with bewilderment. "What is that?"

"You tell me."

"I've never seen that before in my life."

"Haven't you?" he asked.

She shook her head negatively and walked further out onto the porch. "No, I haven't."

John rose from his crouched position, holding the leather innocuously in his hands. He carefully tested the suppleness of it, watching as her gaze followed the action. "I found out something today."

"Did you?" she asked, her eyes still locked on his actions.

"I found out that Daniel Gallows was your biological father," he said, making the statement bluntly, trying to gauge her reaction. He needed to confirm if his instinct was right. He needed to confirm if she was the one responsible for Daniel Gallows's murder.

Mary didn't respond to his words, she seemed shocked. John knew her reaction wasn't due to ignorance of the truth. He had seen her look before. It was the look of a person trapped. He steeled himself against the hurt and panic that had come into her eyes. "Why did you do it Mary? Why did you kill Daniel Gallows?"

She stared at him silently.

"Mary?" he prompted, watching her closely. He

wanted to tell her that her silence was more effective than any words, but he didn't. He knew it was imperative to force her hand. "Talk to me, Mary. Did Gallows threaten you in some way? Did you owe him something that he was trying to collect on?"

His words seemed to break the stunned stupor she had succumbed to. "I didn't owe the man anything."

John thought he detected a slight waver in her voice. He knew that if he pushed even a little bit, she would break. He took a step toward her, to test her resolve, and felt a certain amount of satisfaction when she took a step back. She wasn't as calm as she looked. "Tell me what happened. Was he blackmailing you in some way?"

She shook her head at his words. "You don't know what you're talking about."

John ignored the interruption and continued as if she had not spoken. He didn't want to give her the opportunity to speak. He needed to break her so that she would tell him the truth. And the only way he knew to do that was to keep his words coming fast and furious. It was a tactic that few people could endure. "You had his murder planned down to the last detail, didn't you? You made sure that you had enough guests in place to ensure that we wouldn't be able to pinpoint a definitive suspect. You had three people related to Gallows that had a strong motive to take the man out. You had the opportunity to commit the perfect crime. You were probably watching Gallows the whole night. You knew every move he made. You knew the exact location of his niece throughout the evening. You probably had it staged so that she would find the body. What did you do? Did you plant the seed for her to go and find Gallows after you killed him in an effort to make it look like she committed the crime? Tell me, what did Gallows do that was so heinous that you felt the need to murder him? What exactly was his crime?"

Mary looked at him, cold rage reflected in her eyes. "He killed my father!"

Chapter Twenty

"He killed your father," John repeated, not sure if he had heard her correctly.

"My real father. The only father I ever knew. Daniel Gallows was responsible for pushing him to the edge. As far as I'm concerned, the man effectively murdered him," she ground out, her anger taking control of her words.

John sensed the deep rage that had been building within her, and he kept his tone level and low while he tried to get her to talk. "You knew Daniel Gallows was your biological father all along," he said, his words a statement and not a question.

"I knew. But what's worse, he knew. It was a private adoption. Daniel Gallows threw me away like yesterday's trash."

John watched her carefully as she spoke, feeling her total hatred for the man. Her emotions were that tangible. He had known when he decided to push her that she would break. He didn't expect her to shatter. The

177

words spilled out of her mouth as if they had a will of their own.

Mary expelled a harsh breath. "The Brannigans believed in total honesty. I couldn't have been more than five or six when they told me about the adoption. They even told me who my real father was. I used to see Daniel Gallows ride around town with Christine, but the man never gave me the time of day."

"That had to be rough," John said, trying to instill the right amount of sympathy into his voice. He wanted to keep her talking.

"What was even tougher was that his attitude changed when I was in high school. He wanted a relationship with me at that point."

"Was that why your family moved to Boston?" John asked, guessing that there had to be a reason for the sudden move.

"Yes. The problem was, Daniel Gallows didn't like to be thwarted. He wanted me in his life, regardless of the fact that I didn't want to have anything to do with him," she said, her bitterness over the situation evident in her words, in her body language.

"And he didn't like it when he didn't get his way."

"No, he didn't. He had connections. He called in some favors, and the loans my father had outstanding were called in. But we didn't have the capital to pay off the debt. Pressures began to really mount at that point."

"That was about the time your father committed suicide," John said.

Anger flared in her eyes at his words. "My father would never had taken his own life if it wasn't for Daniel Gallows. The man wouldn't leave us alone.

Daniel Gallows deserved everything that happened. He deserved to know first hand the amount of suffering my father did. How it felt to have the life choked out of you."

"And his eagerness to get close to you gave you the perfect opportunity for revenge," John said, getting a clear picture of how much effort and thought she had put into her plan.

"It really wasn't that hard. The man was just waiting for me to come back into his life. That car," she said, motioning to the sports car that sat in the driveway, "was my welcome home gift."

John's thoughts flashed back to the file they had found at Daniel Gallows's residence with the information on Crosswind, and he recalled Mary's original explanation that the man had expressed an interest in acquiring rights to the property. "That file we found on Crosswind, the one with the financial prospectus, that was a business plan. Daniel Gallows gave you money when you opened this place, didn't he?" John said, thinking about the money they couldn't trace.

"He gave me money," she admitted. "I didn't want it, but he kept insisting. He said to consider it a security blanket in case I ever needed anything. As if I would ever need anything from him. I think he thought that the money would be some kind of tie between us. He thought if I took it, it would mean I was accepting him into my life."

"So you took advantage of his vulnerability toward you. You took the money because it gave you the opening you needed to put your plan into motion. But in order for your plan to work, your relationship with Daniel Gallows had to stay a secret. Nobody could know about it. And nobody did," John said, drawing the conclusion from her words.

"He wasn't about to air his dirty laundry. Everything was done with cold, hard cash. He didn't want Christine to know about me. He didn't think she could handle the truth. She had his undivided attention for so long, he didn't want to say anything to upset her. He said he would tell her when the time was right, but I knew he was lying. He didn't have the guts to admit to his sin. He would never have acknowledged me openly."

"So you had no trouble in taking the man out of the picture."

"No, I didn't," she admitted without remorse just as the loud wail of a police siren pierced the air.

At the sound, John looked toward the street. A patrol car was racing toward Crosswind. He squinted his eyes against the afternoon glare as he tried to see who was in the car. He barely made out Sam's features. John could think of only one explanation for Sam's presence, for the use of the siren. He must have found out something that connected Mary unequivocally to the murder of Daniel Gallows.

John turned back to Mary, maintaining eye contact with her, wondering if she was going to bolt. He didn't think she would, but it wouldn't have surprised him. Not that it would matter. There was nowhere she could go.

"John!" Sam called out as he stepped from the car, his gun drawn.

John briefly glanced at him. "You won't need that," he said, motioning with his chin to the firearm before turning back to Mary.

He handcuffed her before reading her rights. When he was through, he escorted her to the back of the waiting patrol car.

Sam stood back as John slammed the door. "The report came in on the note Mary claimed she received."

John heard just one word. "Claimed?"

"Yeah. I tried to reach you on your cell phone with the results, but I just got voicemail."

"My cell phone's in the car," John admitted. "What did the lab find?"

"Forensics was able to pick up a partial print from the adhesive. It matched Mary's."

"She created the note?"

"There's no other way that her fingerprint could have been where they found it. She had to be the author."

John contemplated Sam's words. "She fabricated evidence," he said, beginning to get an idea of how far Mary was willing to go to lead the investigation away from her.

"It looks that way. And I could think of only one reason for her to have done that. She had to have killed the man," Sam replied. He looked to where Mary sat in the back of the patrol car, staring stoically ahead. "She confessed?"

"Yeah, she cracked under pressure."

"A lot of people do."

"You know, I think she honestly thought she was going to get away with this," John said, making the admission reluctantly. He couldn't believe that he had read the woman so wrongly.

"Everybody who commits a crime thinks they're going to get away with it," Sam reminded him.

John sighed and turned back to face the house which was now overrun with squad cars. "I know."

"Are you okay?"

"Why wouldn't I be?"

"I don't know. I kind of got the impression that you sort of liked Mary."

John ran a weary hand across the back of his neck, kneading the tense muscles. "I did. I do. I know it's strange, but I really feel sorry for her. And she's probably the last person who needs my sympathy. She's more than proven that she can remove any obstacle in her path. She came back to town with deadly intentions, and she carried through on her plan. She had everybody fooled. Myself included. If she didn't give us the note, if I didn't come here this afternoon, she would have gotten away with murder. Literally."

"That's how we solve the cases. By the mistakes of the perps."

John gave a humorless laugh at Sam's description. "Somehow, I never thought of Mary in that regard."

"I know."

"That was my first mistake in handling this case."

"Don't be too hard on yourself. There was a lot of evidence pointing to other people. Paxton especially," Sam said.

"It turns out the only thing Brad Paxton is guilty of is bad judgment. He caused his own problems with that stock transaction."

Sam nodded and looked back toward the street to where a CSI van could be seen turning into the driveway. "It looks like it's time to take this house apart."

John followed Sam's gaze, watching as a technician stepped from the van. He could hear additional sirens in the distance as more emergency vehicles were dispatched to the site to assist with the evidentiary search. "Yeah, but I want to be an active part of the search. I want to make sure that we have all the bases covered to get a conviction. I don't want her to walk because of a technicality."

"I already called Elizabeth and told her not to expect me home tonight."

John nodded and glanced around one final time at the manicured grounds of the estate that had an aura of peace and tranquility. It was a deceptive façade. "Come on. Let's go and take care of business," he murmured before turning to walk into Crosswind.